In the
COMPANY
of WOMEN

In the
COMPANY
of WOMEN

The Story of Joanna

Barbara Anderson

RESOURCE *Publications* · Eugene, Oregon

IN THE COMPANY OF WOMEN
The Story of Joanna

Resource Publications
An Imprint of Wipf and Stock Publishers
199 W. 8th Ave., Suite 3
Eugene, OR 97401

www.wipfandstock.com

PAPERBACK ISBN: 978-1-6667-3702-8
HARDCOVER ISBN: 978-1-6667-9606-3
EBOOK ISBN: 978-1-6667-9607-0

VERSION NUMBER 072622

www.barbandersonauthor.com

For Chris

With him went the Twelve, as well as certain women who had been cured of evil spirits and ailments: Mary the Magdalene, from whom seven demons had gone out, Joanna the wife of Herod's steward Chuza, Susanna, and many others who provided for them out of their own resources.

LUKE 8:1

We call a person the best midwife if she is trained in all branches of therapy. She will be unperturbed, unafraid in danger, able to state clearly the reasons for her measures; she will bring reassurance to her patient, and be sympathetic.

SORANUS, SECOND CENTURY AD

I

The only light in the stone hallway is from the small clay lamp that Anat carries. Heavy iron braziers line the hallway, but other servants have extinguished their light hours before. Her lamp cannot dispel the shadows hovering near the ceiling, but with the small pool of light at her feet, she can at least avoid the benches and chests that line the walls. The palace is so new she can still smell the cut wood of the furniture and feel the grit of newly hewn stone beneath her feet. The swish of her sandals matches the hiss of the wick's flame. Anat is small for a nine-year-old and at first glance appears frail. Her legs and arms are thin, and it is easy to miss the jut of her chin, lifted in determination. She is not afraid of the dark, but she is nervous to wake her mistress, for above all, she needs to do it without disturbing Joanna's husband. Chuza never minded being awakened with orders from the king or messages from the kitchens, but Anat had learned that when Chuza was woken by a servant with a request for his wife, this caused unpleasantness.

She comes to the end of the long hall and places her lamp on the marble table next to the door. Slowly and carefully turning the iron ring in the door's center, she pushes it open. The small flame flickers in the draft. Anat can barely make out the figures in the bed. As her eyes adjust to the dark, she can see that Chuza is lying with his arm flung over his wife as if to pin her to the bed. Joanna is sleeping on her back near the edge of her side of the bed, arms folded at her side. Anat carefully approaches and touches Joanna's foot and Joanna's eyes immediately fly open as if she has been waiting for the merest touch. Her eyes gleam in the faint light, an unspoken question on her face. Anat nods. As Anat turns away, Joanna carefully begins to roll out inch by inch from under her husband's arm. He stirs but does not wake up. Standing, she ties on her sandals and gathers up a cloak from a nearby chair. Anat takes a large, worn leather bag from the corner table and slings it around her neck. Together they leave the room, closing the door softly, pausing to pick up the lamp.

Making their way down the hall, they exit at the far end through the archway of the nearest portico and down the patio steps. An elderly woman accompanied by a soldier stands waiting for them. The guard holds his torch high, his spear gleaming in the light. He gives a slight bow to Joanna. The women confer. "Deborah," Joanna says, "how is Mika's labor progressing"?

The tension on Deborah's face holds the answers before she can utter a word.

"She has labored now for two days, and her womb is still closed. She is near the end of her strength, and death is coming. The only thing we can to do now is to cut the baby out, and you know I don't have the skill. Otherwise, the baby will die too."

"Has Sandor been told?"

"Yes."

"Very well," says Joanna. "Let him call upon the gods of his people. We will turn to ours." Turning to the guard, she says, "Please escort us across the road to the servant quarters."

"Certainly, my lady, and I will inform the next shift to watch for you to be coming back later today." As they walk across the large inner courtyard, Joanna tries to still her apprehension. The crescent moon is bright, and the air is cold. She clutches her cloak up around her throat as she quickly reviews the steps she will need to take for a safe delivery for the child and hopefully for the mother. To calm herself, she thinks back to when she started helping her mother. She was only ten. She smiles faintly as she remembers what a serious and purposeful child she was. They arrive at the main gate. Used to the sight of Joanna and Anat coming and going during the night, the palace guards on the ramparts show no interest. Unlocking a small door to the right of the entrance, the guard allows them to pass through the door and across the wide avenue which runs in front of the palace. On the other side of the road, servant quarters stretch in both directions, disappearing in shadows. Deborah leads them to a small door, and the guard waits while Anat relights her lamp by the torch. Then all three proceed down a low, dank passageway.

As Joanna follows Anat and the elderly midwife, fear and apprehension rise up. Under her cloak, her hands tremble. She reminds herself that she is nineteen, more than old enough and experienced enough to face this challenge. She tries to control her breathing, remembering her mother entering a birthing room, her calm demeanor, her steady hands—always reassuring no matter the amount of blood or cries of pain. Joanna imagines that her mother is with her now, and the thought comforts her. "Being a midwife is a sacred trust," her mother often said. "Breathe and pray, breathe and pray."

The women duck their heads, entering a small, fetid room. With a quick glance, Joanna checks to see what supplies are ready. The small table holds a basin of water, clean cloths, and salt. But then all of her attention focuses on the writhing woman before her on the pallet. Mika's black skin is taut over the enormous mound of her belly, which roils with each contraction. Her face is ashen, and her forehead is crusted with sweat. She no longer has the strength to scream but instead moans and mewls like a cat. She twists and turns. The women beside her attempt to hold her hands and to bathe her face, but she flails wildly, as if trying to escape her own body.

Joanna sinks to her knees and places one ear against the woman's belly. After listening intently for several moments, she examines the vagina, causing the woman to shriek with the additional pain. Joanna stands and places her hands on either side of Mika's face and bends over her. She speaks quietly but firmly. "Mika," she says. "I am here. I am here to cut the baby out, because it can't come out on its own. It is wedged in. We will give you something for the pain, but you must continue to be brave." Turning, she issues a series of quiet instructions. "The baby is still alive but barely moving. We must act swiftly, and maybe we can save them. Anat, lay out my knives, the hyssop, and a needle and threads. Deborah, give her a small dose of the hyssop, but not too much. She is too weak to take a large dose. You women take her hands and shoulders after she falls asleep. She must not be allowed to move as I cut, or there will be too much damage."

Turning, she sees the small bag of salt which has been provided. In order to preserve the amount of water they have for the mother and the baby, Joanna rubs her hands with the salt, swiftly brushing the grains onto the floor. She then opens the small black leather pouch, which Anat already has unpacked. Several tools are inside, and she carefully selects the smallest knife with the shortest blade. She passes the blade through the lamp's flame as she closes her eyes and prays aloud, "Blessed be the God of Israel, who created the world and all that is in it. Remember us, O LORD, as you favor your people; visit us with your saving help."

Mika has sunk into unconsciousness. Taking a deep breath, Joanna says, "Good. She is ready. Deborah, hold her shoulders down, and the two of you each take a leg. Keep her very still. Do not let her move. Anat, stand aside and avert your eyes as I cut into the belly, but be ready to take the child. This is not a sight for your eyes yet."

Joanna places her hand on the woman's belly and locates the position of the baby's head. She and Deborah exchange a long look of apprehension and hope. Joanna carefully but swiftly slices through the abdomen and uterine layers until she reaches the infant. Blood and amniotic fluids gush and seep into the pallet. Placing her hands gently around the baby's shoulders, she eases out the baby's head and upper torso. Deborah uses cloths and pressure to stem the flow of blood. With her little finger, Joanna wipes out the blood and fluids from the baby's nose and mouth before she lifts the entire baby from the womb. As she cuts the umbilical cord, the baby starts to cry.

Deborah and Joanna exchange wide smiles. "Take the baby, Anat. Clean and swaddle him. Blessed be the LORD, the God of Israel."

"Blessed be the God of Israel," echo the other women. Anat rubs the baby's body with salt, removing the fluids, and washes his head and face with a damp cloth. Joanna reminds her about the umbilical cord. She covers the end of the umbilical cord with olive oil and then lays a clean cloth over it. She then swaddles the baby, and his cries cease as she walks him up and down.

The woman swiftly work to deliver the placenta in order to stop the bleeding as soon as possible. Deborah bends over the body, holding the layers together as Joanna starts to stitch up the womb layer by layer, taking exacting care. Long minutes go by as the stitching continues and the womb and abdomen are closed. Before they can finish, Mika floats back to consciousness, and the helpers have to struggle to keep her still. Mika's eyes latch onto Joanna. Joanna reassures her. "Your baby has been born. You have been blessed with a son. He is warm and well and will be in your arms soon, but you must hold as still as you can and endure. I will work as swiftly as I can." The woman's eyes flow with tears, but she smiles as her son starts to cry.

Finishing the stitching, Deborah and Joanna straighten up slowly, easing their backs. Deborah pours olive oil over the stitches, and Joanna examines the wound carefully for any sign of angry redness or seepage. The attendants give Mika water and place a fresh pallet beneath her. Joanna gently winds a long, narrow cloth under her body and over the stitching. Mika falls into a deep sleep, but the grayness is already leaving her face. She is too weak to nurse, but Anat tucks the baby in next to her, and soon the baby is asleep too. As Anat packs up the leather bag, the women consult together about how best to help the mother nurse while protecting the stitches. Joanna then lists precautions that need to be taken against sickness and fever. "Only broth for the next few days. She must not be allowed to get up for the next two weeks. Check the womb twice a day, and call for Deborah immediately if she starts to run a fever. Unfortunately, I am traveling to Capernaum tomorrow, so I won't be available to help."

After exchanging embraces all around, Joanna and Anat leave wearily, their cloaks over their arms. Pausing at the entrance to the servant quarters, they wait to allow a line of market-bound donkeys to go by. It is midmorning, and heat swims in the small clouds of dust. The smell of fresh dung is strong and makes Joanna aware of her own dishevelment and sweat. Suddenly weary, she sags against the doorpost. She smiles ruefully at Anat and says, "Both of us have had quite a night. I don't think I have enough strength to walk a step. You must be exhausted too."

Anat nods, but after a moment she clutches Joanna's elbow and draws her across the street, past the guards at the gate and into the vast courtyard, stopping several yards from the massive central well. Joanna motions to a servant nearby, who brings them a ladle of water. They hold out two small wooden cups they carry at their belts. The servant fills their small cups to the brim. They both drink deeply, and then drink again.

The life of the palace swirls around them. Soldiers who have finished their shift report to the daily officer before heading to their barracks. A small crowd of boys delivers baskets of faggots and dried dung to the entrance of the kitchen building. As usual, there is an argument about payment between the boys and the assistant cook. Joanna and Anat smile at the familiar sight. A stray dog slinks into the courtyard to lick up any water that has splashed from the well. A servant shoos it away. Joannna notices her husband's servants carrying messages to the stables and the palace warehouse. But of Chuza himself, there is no sign.

II

After several moments, Joanna and Anat get up, cross the courtyard, and approach a limestone archway that leads to the mikvah. Going down wide steps, they enter the preparation room, where the attendant awaits. "What a mess! You are both filthy," she clucks. "It must have been a difficult birth." Briskly, she helps them disrobe, taking care not to touch any cloth with blood on it. She assures Joanna that their change of clothes has been delivered. "You both look exhausted. Let's get you cleaned off right away."

"First, can you send word to Sandor? Tell him that his wife had a very difficult birth but is resting now and that he has a son."

The attendant waves her young helper away to run the errand. Then she leads Joanna and Anat to a low stone trough. They disrobe, leaving their clothes puddled on the floor. Filling her jar over and over again, the attendant sluices them with water, making sure that every inch of them has been rinsed. As Joanna feels the water pour over her head and shoulders, she begins to relax and holds out her hands for extra attention. The attendant scrubs her fingernails with a small brush and cleans under each nail, then sluices her again. She repeats the procedure for Anat. Then the attendant wraps each of them with a towel and leads them down a small hall to the mikvah pool. The pool is hewn out of stone, and wide steps lead into the water from all four sides. The surface of the water ripples as spring water constantly renews the freshness of the water. There are no windows in the mikvah, but there is an opening cut into the roof. Dust motes drift on the eddies of air. The noise from the courtyard is deadened by the thick walls and the slight lap of the water. It is the most peaceful spot in the whole palace.

Joanna's tiredness begins to seep away. She begins the traditional prayer: "Blessed are you, God, Majestic Spirit of the Universe, who make us holy by embracing us in living waters. And blessed are you, Source of All Life, who keep us alive and sustain us and enable us to reach this day."

As she immerses herself in the water, she sinks down completely, staying underwater for a long moment, and Anat does the same. Then they both stand. Joanna uses both hands to lift and smooth her hair from her face. She tilts her face into the shaft of sunlight and enjoys its brightness. Water runs down her strong shoulders and long limbs. They climb the steps. Pausing, they bend and both wring the water from their hair. The attendant then wraps them again in their towels and leads them back to the preparation room. She hands Joanna a a wide-tooth comb. As Joanna combs and braids Anat's hair, the attendant combs and braids Joanna's hair. Curious and wanting to know all the details, the attendant asks, "So the birthing was difficult?"

Joanna smiles and nods. "It was very difficult, but both Mika and her son have survived. Pray that there is no infection or fever. It is in the LORD's hands. His will be done."

"His will be done," agrees the attendant. "Sandor will be so happy. Whenever he has had a free moment, he has been pacing up and down the courtyard." Taking the towels, she hands them their clean clothes.

Joanna and Anat dress. "Thank you for your kind attentions," Joanna says. "God will reward your service to his people." She bows slightly, and the attendant returns the gesture. Anat shoulders the leather medical bag once again.

As they turn to go, the attendant asks, motioning to Anat, "When do you think this one will finally start to talk?"

Joanna looks at Anat, who has shrunk back at the critical comment. Frowning, Joanna says, "She doesn't need to talk; she only needs to understand what is needed."

The attendant accepts the mild reprimand and pats Anat goodbye in apology.

Chuza is having his midday meal when Joanna and Anat finally step up under the portico outside of their palace apartment. It is a pool of coolness after the heated stones of the courtyard. Slender stone pillars hold up a roof of wooden latticework. Mature grapevines grow in huge clay jars. Twisting and thrusting upwards, they intertwine around the pillars and up into the lattice, forming a thick, shady roof. Grapes hang down, and their fragrance reminds Joanna of how hungry she is. She smiles at Chuza, who is enjoying the bread, cheese, and fruit placed before him. He is ripping pieces of bread from the loaf and chewing them with gusto, washing them down with new wine.

Anat goes and stands next to Sandor, who is attending his master. Unlike most days, Sandor's usually taciturn face is wreathed in smiles. He grins at Joanna and brings her a plate as she seats herself next to her husband. He pours her a glass of wine and then steps aside.

Chuza looks at Joanna. "Wife, I rose early this morning to greet you, but to my surprise you were not there."

"I was summoned to—"

Chuza interrupts. "Yes, that is all well and good, but I found your absence disconcerting. It is not a feeling I enjoy. The details of your nocturnal trips do not interest me."

As he speaks, Joanna is embarrassed that Sandor is hearing how little Chuza cares for his wife and child, and she feels a familiar sadness.

Chuza continues. "I wanted to discuss tomorrow's journey with you. As you know, we were planning to leave for my brother's house tomorrow, but I have received word that there is a caravan from Jaffa arriving in the next several days. I must be here to supervise the unloading of the king's goods, so you will have to go without me. But I still want you to go. I want you to take the foodstuff and supplies my brother's family has requested."

"Your mother will not be pleased to see me arrive without you," she says. "I will be a poor substitute."

Shoving his plate away, Chuza indicates absentmindedly that Sandor take his plate and the tray of food. Joanna starts to protest that she hasn't eaten but then sinks back into her chair.

"My mother and brother understand very well my duty to the king," Chuza says, popping one last grape into his mouth. "Plan on leaving early." He rises and leaves the room without another word.

After a moment, Sandor fetches the tray of food back again and serves Joanna bread, fruit, and cheese. She starts eating as fast as she can in case Chuza returns. She also places some food in a napkin and motions for Sandor to give it to Anat.

As he refills her wine glass, Sandor says softly, "Many, many thanks. Because of you, we have been given a son. The gods are smiling on us."

"You are welcome Sandor, but it is our one LORD who is great and good, all-powerful and merciful. It is he who guided my hands. Blessed be the LORD forever. But you and Deborah need to keep a close watch. This is a dangerous time for mother and son. Mika lost so much blood, and she is very weak. Her wound can easily become infected, and you know that babies can catch fever so easily. I will have Chuza give a message to the kitchen that she will not be able to work for many weeks. She needs to rest and let her body heal."

"We will take every care," Sandor says, taking the tray. Joanna picks up her wine glass and drinks the rest of the watered wine as she walks through the apartment into their bedroom. Anat follows, still eating her bread and fruit. Without disrobing and after taking a last sip of wine, Joanna sinks onto the bed and falls fast asleep. Anat finishes her bread, takes off the leather bag, and lays it on the table. She curls up on her pallet in the corner and listens to her mistress's steady breathing. Soon, she is asleep too.

The next day quite early, three male servants lead Joanna's small horse and five laden donkeys out the main gate of the palace. As Joanna and Anat cross the courtyard to meet them, Chuza walks with them, giving them instructions. "Please give my brother my regrets for missing the visit." Reaching the animals, Chuza pats the largest bundle on the donkey. "This contains Egyptian cloth for my mother and sister-in-law." Chuza gestures toward the large jars hanging from the second donkey. "And these, of course, are the containers of my brother's favorite wine and the new olive oil. And then there is the cheese and the fruit and other food."

"I will let them know how disappointed you are to not be able to deliver them yourself," Joanna says. She smiles at Chuza, but he doesn't notice.

"I'm sending these two servants with you, which should prevent any unpleasantness on the road. The main road to Capernaum is usually quite safe, so I'm sure that two stout men with staffs will be sufficient. I will look for you to be back in five days." He looks at her coolly. "Please do whatever you can to be of use to my family." Chuza nods to the servants in dismissal and returns to the courtyard. Joanna turns and looks after him wistfully.

Joanna turns to her small brown horse, pats it, and offers it a bit of flatbread. One of the servants helps her mount and then takes up the reins to lead the small group down the street. Looking back, Joanna sees Anat trudging behind the smallest donkey. Calling a halt, she asks that Anat be seated behind the wine jars. The group starts up again, past the palace walls and through the din and business of the main market. Even though it is early, most of the stalls already have customers. They head down the crowded thoroughfare and out the main gate of the walled city. As they pass, the soldiers acknowledge their departure while checking carefully all those who are entering.

Two days later, the women and children of Jairus's household are having lunch. Joanna is sitting with her mother-in-law, Rebecca; her sister-in-law, Phoebe; and her nieces and nephews. It is hot even under the shade of the two trees in the courtyard, but there is a slight breeze from the water. The heat saps the appetites of the women, who only pick at their meal, but the children eat heartily, as usual. The small fountain nearby gurgles. Anat and an elderly household servant serve the meal. Gazing at her mother and sister-in-law, Joanna again notices the contrast between Phoebe and Rebecca. Phoebe is as plump and self-satisfied as a prized pigeon. She has a languid nature and sinks heavily into the cushions. She fusses at the children from time to time, but with no real purpose. Sure of Jairus's regard for her, she contentedly reigns over their prosperous household. Rebecca, on the other hand, is thin, with a permanent scowl on her face, her wrinkles deeply etched. She is a nervous woman, always plucking the folds of her tunic and adjusting her necklaces. The role of mother-in-law does not sit well with her, and Joanna knows that the current truce between the two may not last through lunch.

After staring a long moment at Anat, Rebecca says, "Joanna, I must admit I still find her silence unnerving. Don't you find it strange that she never talks? I can't imagine why Chuza chose her for you. I can never tell what she is thinking. Surely you could find a more suitable attendant."

Joanna demurs. "She is a good worker and has been with me so long I no longer notice her silence. Besides, she is helpful in my work and is never sick or squeamish."

Rebecca and Phoebe make small expressions of distaste.

"But that ugly bag," says Phoebe, "why is it always around her neck?

Joanna smiles at Anat. "She prefers to carry my medical supplies herself. And after all, we never know when we might need what's inside."

Phoebe turns her mind to other matters and addresses her children. "I'm sorry you could not hear the preacher yesterday, but it was right to leave you home."

Rebecca nods in agreement. "Joanna, it was good for you to oversee the children. If you ever have any of your own, you will need to know how to handle them. You have been married what? Four years? It's high time you set aside birthing others' babies and settled down to motherhood yourself."

Not to be left out, Phoebe adds, "Jairus says that Chuza is getting quite impatient." Joanna hides how these familiar refrains hurt her. Keeping her face still, she busies herself by pulling her smallest niece onto her lap and feeding her a dried fig.

Phoebe makes a wry face. "It certainly was no place for children. The crowd covered the whole hillside. Many of them were from outside the city, and they were noisy, unruly . . ."

". . . and smelly," interjects Rebecca.

Phoebe continues, "But of course, there were important people there too. All of the priests and officials from our synagogue were there, as well as some Pharisees from Judea. Jesus is beginning to have quite a reputation, Jairus says."

"Surely he is a powerful teacher. We have even heard of him in Tiberius," Joanna comments. "What did he preach about? Was it so very different than what rabbis and priests usually say?"

Phoebe shakes her head. "Well, I didn't understand most of it. Something about 'blessed are the poor in spirit' and 'blessed are those who mourn'—whatever that means."

"Don't forget," says Rebecca, "he also compared the crowds to salt and light. As if that crowd was capable of anything besides complaining and wondering where their next meal was coming from."

Joanna glances up from feeding her niece and catches the women exchanging self-satisfied smiles. She detects some kind of excitement and knows that something out of the ordinary is being planned.

Casually, Phoebe says, "Speaking of meals, Joanna—Jairus has invited the Nazarene to attend a dinner here in his honor tomorrow." Casting aside her attempt at calm, she practically squeals, "And he has agreed to come. The other officials' wives are so jealous. I'm sure we will need places for twenty or more. I know that it won't be like the feasts at the palace in Tiberius, but we will do our best." Joanna is happy that Phoebe and Rebecca are so pleased, and she immediately offers her help.

Phoebe continues. "Here in Capernaum, it would not be proper for the women of the family to attend, so we will eat separately. But Joanna, we need to make an exception for you—not to sit down at the meal, of course, but we need you to take charge of the serving, since you know how these things should be done. The servants always need supervision. And double-check with Jairus about the seating arrangements; it would not do to cause offense. Jesus will be at the head table, of course, but other placements might be complicated. The Pharisees who are attending will be most particular. Everything must be perfect. I will take care of the menu. It is a good thing you brought so many special supplies from Tiberius."

Joanna nods in agreement and then starts to worry about meeting such high expectations. "You know, I don't actually attend the feasts at the palace," she demurs.

Phoebe waves her hand in dismissal. "I'm sure you will do fine. Just keep an eye on the servants and make sure everything goes smoothly. When you are not needed, you can wait behind the archway out of sight."

After an evening of receiving numerous instructions about the serving of the meal and watching Phoebe and Rebecca discuss and disagree with one another, Joanna gratefully goes to her room. Anat has unpacked her things and is asleep on her mat at the foot of the bed. Before going to bed, Joanna takes several deep breaths and tries not to imagine all the different mistakes she might make at the dinner. More than ever, she wishes that Chuza were there.

He has a way with his mother and can usually humor her out of any sulk. And he certainly could make sure all parts of the dinner went smoothly. Joanna smiles a wry smile. "I certainly am a poor substitute," she thinks to herself.

The next night, Joanna surveys the courtyard. After last-minute fussing and with a flurry of instructions, Rebecca, Phoebe, and the maidservants disappear into the house. All is in readiness. The stars hang low in the sky. The aroma of roasted meat and spices fills the warm air. A servant stands at the gate ready to receive guests, and another begins to bring out dishes from the kitchen. Four low tables are placed at the western end of the courtyard in an open rectangle. The fourth table is slightly separated from the others. Each corner of the courtyard has a tall iron stand holding a bright lantern. Small oil lamps dot the tables, and fat brown and gold cushions provide seating. At each table, blocks of wood are placed to hold the communal bowls. Tonight they will be filled with mutton stew and mixed grains. Platters of flatbreads, small bowls of olive oil for dipping, and platters of braised lentil and onion are already placed in easy reach. On a serving table along the wall are spouted decanters full of the wine Joanna has brought from Tiberius. Plates of fruit and cheese are arranged in artful patterns, ready for the end of the meal.

Jairus strides into the courtyard. Bursting with excitement and goodwill, he approaches Joanna, rubbing his hands nervously and smiling. He is shorter than Chuza but with the same sturdy frame. "Well, my brother is going to be jealous when he learns that he missed all this. Everything looks ready. You have done a good job. Phoebe and I are grateful for all your help."

Joanna grins back at him. His open face reminds her of when Chuza used to grin at her in exactly that same way. Both men have inherited the wiriness of their mother and the sturdiness of their father, but Jairus has the soft hands and the belly of an administrator. In contrast, Chuza's work has kept his hands calloused and his shoulders muscled.

Minutes later, the guests start to arrive at the main gate. The local synagogue officials and town leaders arrive first. They dip their hands in the fresh water provided, and Joanna signals to the nearby servant to seat them at the far tables. The murmur of voices begins as the wine is poured and sampled. The visiting Pharisees arrive, and the locals turn and try to be subtle about their curiosity while still taking in every detail of their appearance. The prayer shawls of the men are immaculate, and the lengthy tassels that fringe the ends are scrupulously tied with blue cord. As Jairus bustles up to greet them, they daintily wash their fingers, the leather straps of their phylacteries winding up their left arms. Jairus conscientiously seats them near the head table. The head Pharisee, of course, is ushered to the left of Jairus's own place. Nervously, Jairus pours the head Pharisee's wine himself and makes some comments about the weather. Joanna stands by the side table readying the first course, and another servant scuttles to the kitchen to fetch an overlooked serving ladle. And so it is that the Nazarene arrives and receives no greeting. As Joanna turns around, she glimpses him at the entrance to the courtyard. He is waiting patiently for his host to notice him.

"This Nazarene is not so very impressive," she thinks. "He is not tall. I was expecting a larger-than-life figure. He is neither pale nor dark, and his beard needs a trim." Suddenly, she smiles to herself, thinking, "I could be describing myself. I'm neither this nor that. There is nothing remarkable about me either. We are the same, except that it is my hair that needs trimming, not my beard." She smiles at her own silliness. In contrast to the Pharisees, Jesus' robe is plain over a rough chiton, and his sandals are worn. His hands are rough and calloused and loosely folded. But then Joanna becomes aware of the silence which surrounds Jesus. It is as if he is wrapped in a mantle of stillness.

All this flashes through her mind as she starts across the courtyard to greet him. At the same time, Jairus turns and realizes that Jesus has arrived. Embarrassed, he rushes past her and, grabbing both of Jesus' arms, leads him to the head table. "Welcome, welcome," he says. Jesus is seated on Jairus's right and the head Pharisee on his left. The Pharisee gives Jesus a long look, and Jesus smiles back. Jesus takes a sip of wine and compliments Jairus on its flavor.

Jairus stands to make a small welcome speech and waits until the guests have quieted. "Esteemed neighbors and guests, my house is blessed with your presence. Behold how good it is, and how pleasant, when men break bread together. Give thanks to the LORD, for he is good."

And all the guests reply, "His mercy endures forever."

Jairus offers a short blessing over the food, and the feast begins. Along with the mutton stew, a platter of veal is delivered to the head table. Jairus slices pieces of the thigh and makes sure Jesus and the Pharisee receive the choicest bits. Both men nod their thanks. For the moment, everyone is occupied with their food and wine.

But soon, the head Pharisee's voice is heard above the sound of eating. Many at the other tables quiet down, looking forward to the discussion they know is coming. They want to feast on the debate just as much as on the roasted meat. They know the Pharisees object to much of Jesus' teaching, and this is an opportunity to hear the arguments for themselves. While keeping an eye on those serving the food, Joanna edges closer, wanting to hear also.

The head Pharisee raises his voice so all can hear. He is anxious to assert his authority to the assembled group. "Yesterday, Jesus, you said that blessed are the poor in spirit, for the kingdom of heaven is theirs. Surely you do not mean to imply that you know what God's will is."

"Yes, I do." His voice is rich and low and carries well in the night air. Calmly, he continues eating.

Realizing that Jesus is not going to say anything else, the Pharisee objects, "But is it not written that God's favor is for the righteous? For those who follow the law? Our teachings say nothing about the poor in spirit."

Jesus smiles and puts down his goblet of wine. He folds his hands into his sleeves and leans back. "Well, let me tell a story." All keep eating, but everyone stops talking. Stories are good, often better than debate. "Two men went up to the temple to pray, one

Pharisee"—Jesus bows at his challenger—"and the other a tax collector. The Pharisee stood by himself and prayed: 'Lord, I thank you that I am not like the other people—or even like this tax collector. I fast twice a week and give a tenth of all I receive.'" The Pharisees look at one another and nod in approval. The Pharisee at the head table returns Jesus' bow.

Jesus continues. "But the tax collector stood at a distance. He would not even look up to heaven but beat his breast and said, 'God, have mercy on me, a sinner.' I tell you that this man, rather than the other, went home justified before God."

The Pharisees squirm with embarrassment at the unexpected turn in the story, and Jairus is dismayed. As Jesus starts to eat again, the rest of the guests murmur and mumble to one another—some agreeing with Jesus, some not. Joanna looks at Jairus and knows that he is trying to figure out a way to salvage the awkward situation, a way to mollify the Pharisees without insulting his guest, but nothing is coming to mind.

Just then, Joanna becomes aware that two women have entered the courtyard through the open doorway. One woman is simply but richly dressed. Her hair is covered with a thin linen cloth, and the bracelets on her wrists signal a woman of stature and means. Her eyes snap with intelligence. The other woman is barefoot and dressed only in a homespun shift. Her black hair is unbound and uncovered. It cascades down her back. Joanna notices that her belly mounds underneath the rough fabric. She is weeping and carrying a small flask in shaking hands. Joanna swiftly crosses the courtyard to stop the interruption before anyone else notices. The presence of the women will ruin the dinner, scandalizing the guests. But the weeping woman sees Jesus at the head table and starts to rush toward him. Joanna reaches out to stop her, but the other woman catches her arm and draws her back. "Peace, my lady," she says. "We will be gone in a moment."

As the woman throws herself at Jesus' feet, her sobbing grows louder. The guests are shocked into silence. As she cries, she anoints his feet with ointment, kisses them, and dries them with her hair. After several moments of stunned disbelief, Jairus struggles to his feet and begins to try to pull her away. "Woman, what are you doing? Leave this instant. This is no place for you. Leave—leave at once!"

Jesus waves him back and places his hand on the woman's head as if to protect her. He doesn't shout, but everyone can hear him. "Do you see this woman? When I entered your house, you did not give me water for my feet, but she has bathed them with her tears. You did not anoint my head with oil, but she has anointed me with costly fragrance. I tell you, her many sins have been forgiven, because she has shown great love."

At these words, the shocked silence erupts, and some onlookers shake their fists and complain at the brazenness of the women. Others object to Jesus' words. In the tumult, the two women slip away.

The Pharisees and synagogue leaders begin to chastise Jesus. "Only God has the power to forgive sin!" "Who do you think you are? This is blasphemy." "This woman is obviously a prostitute."

Jesus stands, and again it seems to Joanna that he wraps himself in stillness. It's as if he does not even hear or see the anger directed at him. Unaffected by the criticisms flung at him, he looks at Jairus, whose face is flush with embarrassment and anger. "Thank you for your hospitality. I will leave you to your other guests. I seem to have caused a disturbance, and I am sorry. Peace be with you."

As Jesus leaves the courtyard, he passes by Joanna, who is still stunned by what has happened. She meets his eyes, but then embarrassed, she looks down. Jesus pauses and says, "Thank you for serving a delicious meal."

When she looks up again, Jesus is gone. The guests continue to argue and debate, reluctant to leave a good dinner. Jairus is crestfallen, and the head Pharisee commiserates with him about the dangers of itinerant preachers and their false teachings. The wine begins to soothe outraged feelings. Inside the house, Rebecca and Phoebe hear the tumult and nervously wait for the feast to be over so that they can find out what has happened. It is obvious that all has not gone well.

I V

S everal days later, Joanna and Anat arrive back in Tiberius. The return trip has been quicker, since the donkeys have fewer burdens. Anat has her donkey all to herself and has spent most of the trip dozing, draped over the donkey's warm neck.

As the servants lead the animals away, a guard appears. "Lady, my lord Chuza is waiting for you. He asked that I bring you to him as soon as you arrived."

Joanna nods wearily. As she trudges across the courtyard, she reminds Anat that they need to check in on Mika later that afternoon. When she and Anat enter the portico, Joanna can see that Chuza is talking animatedly with a woman she does not know. She is laughing, and Joanna can see that she is quite young, with dainty hands and feet. Her husband and the girl are being watched closely by two older women who sit in one corner. Joanna does not recognize the older women either and wonders why they are visiting. She nods a greeting, but the women ignore her. Chuza sees Joanna and immediately stops smiling. He gets up, walks around the table, and stops in front of her. His stance is wide, and his arms are crossed in front of his chest. Joanna is confused and waits for an introduction to the guests. Instead, Chuza states, "While you were gone, I made a decision that concerns you. It is not an easy decision but a necessary one. I am taking a new wife, and this is she."

Joanna stares at Chuza, not grasping the words or their meaning. "I don't understand. What are you saying?"

"I am taking a new wife. I need a son, and because you are barren, I divorce you, as is my right according to the law."

"Chuza, stop!" Fear rises in her as she begins to understand. She reaches out to touch his arm. "We are a family. Look here—I have messages here from your mother and brother." Chuza doesn't respond. "And I have so much news to tell you." Chuza glares at her, stone-faced.

Confused, she begins to beg. "We have only been married four years. The LORD will bless us with a child, I am sure of it. I love you. This is our home!"

"We are not a family. We have no children, and I must have a son. I have waited and waited."

"Please, Chuza, don't! Haven't I done all that I can for your well-being and comfort?"

"Well, I see I must spell it out to you. Joanna, you are not in my bed when I've expressly told you I want you there." Joanna begins to remonstrate, but Chuza cuts her off. "You go about the palace at all hours of the day and night, often improperly dressed. It is an embarrassment to me that you don't know your place. I'm sorry, but my mind is made up. You have been a good wife in some ways, except for the most important. Has the irony never occurred to you? The midwife who can't have children?" he says sarcastically.

Joanna's fear turns to panic. "Yes, I know. Every day I pray to the LORD to bless us. Surely he will hear my pleas and I will be pregnant soon. Please, please be patient."

Chuza remains implacably silent.

Desperation seizes her. "But Chuza, I have nowhere to go. I have no family anymore. You cannot cast me aside. You cannot be as cruel as this. Where will I go?"

"Well, that is no longer my concern. According to the law, you have forfeited the terms of our marriage contract." He turns to the table and, picking up a quill, dips it in ink and voids the contract. Joanna reaches out to stop him, but the watching guard pulls her back. "You may take this pouch containing your ketubah monies with you when you leave. It is all there. I insist that you leave as soon as possible."

Chuza glances back at his new bride, aware that she is listening. Wanting to appear generous in front of her, Chuza continues.

"But I am not without compassion. Accompanied, you can return to our rooms and collect your clothes and such. Whatever you can carry you can keep, but as of this moment I divorce you. We are no longer husband and wife. You will receive your ketubah portion as you leave." He nods to the guard and indicates that he is to follow and watch Joanna.

"But Chuza . . ."

"Go."

Minutes later, Joanna stands stunned in the middle of what used to be her bedroom. The guard stands near the doorway, Anat beside him. As Joanna looks around the room—the bed, the chests, the table—a cold, hard anger slowly takes the place of her shock. Anat reaches out to touch her arm, but Joanna pushes her away. She begins to pace. She snatches up garments and throws them down. She shoves chairs. She strips the bed. The guard grabs her arms and waits until she stops struggling. He lets her go, and she stands trembling in the middle of the room, unaware of the tears flowing down her face. Anat crouches in front of her, clutching her robe, trying to calm her.

As if in a stupor, Joanna whispers, "Leave me. I am discarded . . . replaced. I am nothing. My mother and father are dead. I have no one." Her voice trails off. "There is no future for me. All my friends are here. The LORD has abandoned me."

The guard approaches again. "My lady, if there is nothing you want to take with you, we should go."

Joanna still doesn't move. But Anat rises and readjusts the medical bag around her neck. She then takes another pouch and begins to scoop up all of Joanna's bracelets and necklaces from the side table. She sweeps the brush, comb, and jars of ointment in too. Moving faster, she opens a trunk with a clang and lifts out several cloaks. The clang brings Joanna out of her daze. Her eyes narrow. She takes the pouch from Anat and walks over to Chuza's side of the bed and angrily sweeps all of his jewelry and small ornaments into the bag too. She glares defiantly at the guard, but he does not stop her. She grabs some of Chuza's belts from a nearby chest and fastens then over her waist. She then puts on the two garments and a cloak. She turns to Anat. "Anat," she demands, "give me my medical bag." Anat clutches it and vehemently shakes her head no. Joanna tugs on it. "Now stop it! Give me my bag." Anat backs into a corner, frantically shaking her head. Finally, in frustration, Joanna sweeps her up and the pouch full of belongings and stalks out of the room.

Ungainly because of all the extra clothes, she walks past Chuza and his bride, still carrying Anat. She snatches her bag of coins off the table and sticks it in her cloak pocket. When Chuza realizes how much she has packed to take, he rises to object but subsides when he realizes that his new bride is watching. Stoically, Joanna walks past the well, past curious onlookers, and past the guards at the main gate. She looks to see if anyone is following her, but no one is. Burdened with the bags and the extra clothes, she puts Anat down as they enter the main road. She looks around her, her energy suddenly gone, her mind a blank. She is shocked and immobile, unable to decide what to do next. A man and his donkey pass by on their way to the marketplace with a load of dates. Almost without thinking, Joanna follows him. Anat scurries after her.

The main marketplace is full of stalls, fronted by tables, and shaded with hides or cloths. They contain every variety of food, household item, cloth, and spice. There are used-clothes stalls with their goods displayed on long poles like makeshift flags. Live birds caw, squawk, coo, and chirp in their wooden cages. Storekeepers of sweets arrange their goods by color, and the money lenders sit patiently by their weights and measurements. There are perfume and jewelry vendors also. Woodworkers and potters take orders. It is a raucous place full of haggling voices, arguments, and the shrieks of playing children. Sheep and goats add to the commotion as they are driven through the marketplace to the corrals next to the city walls.

Joanna walks in a stupor, hardly aware of anything around her. At this time in the afternoon, the market is full and the customers jostle with one another and vie for the attention of the shop owners. It is so crowded that she has to grab Anat's hand so that they aren't separated. They practically walk the whole length of the market before she stops at an entrance to an alleyway, places her bundles on the ground, and sits with her back against a wall. Anat squats near her. She keeps looking at Joanna, worried and upset. Joanna's face flushes. Waves of embarrassment and anger wash over her. She remembers how pleased her parents were when Chuza offered marriage. They were so sure that he would provide a loving, stable home, and at the palace no less! She remembers the languid summer nights when they were first married and how Chuza said she was much too pretty to be a midwife. That he would cherish her and dress her in gold bracelets and fine linens. Now all that is gone in the blink of an eye. Joanna feels like a fool. All those women in the teachings who prayed to the LORD for a child were answered. Why not her? She covers her face with her hands, tears streaming down her face.

Gradually, Joanna becomes aware of Anat pressing against her side, patting her arm. She looks around and realizes that the afternoon is well along. Wearily, she trudges to the inn closest to the main gate, with Anat trailing behind. Asking for a room, she fishes in her pocket for the bag of coins to pay the innkeeper, but her pocket is empty! Frantically, she searches all their belongings, but it's nowhere to be found. The crowds in the marketplace . . . the jostling. Somewhere, somehow, someone else has her money. It was all that she had. The innkeeper smirks at her distress and shoos her away.

Joanna sinks down to sit on a long bench along the city wall. Her despair is deep and her anger runs hot, and the more she thinks, the angrier she gets. Her thoughts rail against Chuza, against the thief, against God, who has made her barren—even against her parents, who have died and left her all alone. She hopes that the pickpocket's hand shrivels and falls off! She hopes that Chuza's manhood shrivels too!

Gradually, the smell of roasting vegetables and baking bread makes her realize how late it is. She looks at Anat and begins to shake off her lethargy and rage. Thinking out loud, she mutters, "We somehow need to get more money. Let me think. First, the jewelers . . . I'll take off all these extra clothes I have on and then put on my finest cloak. That way, I won't look like a thief trying to sell stolen jewelry." She thinks for several minutes. "I will make up a story about a doting second husband who doesn't want me wearing anything from my first husband, so he wants me to get rid of all my old rings and bracelets." She continues, "Then we will go to a used-clothes stall and sell the cloaks, belts, and other extra clothes we have. We'll purchase secondhand cloaks and other clothes that we will need. We need to be careful. We can't travel the roads looking like we are so prosperous that we have something to steal, and we can't travel the roads looking so destitute that we will be set upon. We have to be as careful as possible from now on. We need to look poor but respectable, like we are on our way home to a family on a nearby farm." Anat nods her head.

An hour later, Joanna and Anat are eating cheese and bread. There is some shade outside the city walls, and they crouch there, surrounded by their new belongings. Even though she has gone to and from the city many times, none of the soldiers at the gate have recognized her.

After they eat, Joanna still sits as if in a daze. Anat rises and tugs on her arm.

"Yes, yes, it is time to go. But where should we go?"

Anat points down the road.

"Yes, and I know we have to get off this main road as soon as possible." She looks with dismay at the small piles around them. Finally, she picks up the large strapped basket and begins to pack. After a small tussle with Anat, she places her leather medical bag and the several small pouches of coins on the bottom of the basket. "We need to hide our most important belongings if we can," she says in response to Anat's disapproving face. Over it, she puts two small blankets, their extra clothes, candles, and a small flask of water. Joanna hoists the basket over one shoulder, and Anat carries the satchel with their food, bowls, and a pot. Having kept one of the knives from the medical bag out, Joanna places it at her waist under her belt.

They set off walking. About two miles down the road, a track turns to the west. Hoping that the track will lead to nearby farms where they can get work, Joanna turns and follows it into the hills. As the sun goes down, they still have not found a farm or even an abandoned hut. They take shelter at the foot of a tree among some boulders. They curl up in their cloaks and under their blankets and use the bag and basket as pillows. Joanna is so tired she can't even cry. But anxiety keeps her awake, and it is a long time before she sinks into an uneasy doze, her hands wrapped tightly around the straps of the basket.

Dawn wakes them with light and chilly air. With numbed fingers, they eat a breakfast of olives and bread. Joanna finally stirs as anger washes over her again. Jumping up, she paces back and forth, cursing Chuza and their situation. Anat sits huddled next to their belongings. Gradually, Joanna calms down and starts to think. "Anat, get the needles and thread from the leather bag, and I will tear this cloth into smaller pieces. We need to sew small pouches to put our coins in, and then we will sew them into our skirts. Each pouch should have a small bit of cloth wrapped around the coins so that they don't make any noise. If we wear the pouches around our necks, others will be able to see that we are carrying something, so we will hide them under our clothes. You must never let anyone else know that we have them."

Anat nods in understanding and agreement. As she sews, Joanna's stomach clenches once again with embarrassment and anger, her thoughts churning. Finally, she blurts out, "Where is God now? Where is our kind and gracious God? To be cast aside—it is humiliating. How could Chuza do this to me? I won't be able to be a midwife, because who will trust me now? I have no friends, no community." She turns to Anat. "And what about you? How will I take care of you?" She glares at Anat and spits out, "I never should have picked you up and walked out with you. We will slowly starve to death."

Stricken, Anat tries hard not to cry, but she cannot control her tears. Joanna is so caught up in her own feelings it is several minutes before she notices the anguish on Anat's face. Finally, she says, "Anat, did you sleep?" Anat shrugs and starts to sew. Joanna tries in some small way to make up for her violent words. "Perhaps when we get to a farm, they can take you in. I know I can convince them that you are a hard worker. It would be good if you could work for a nice family." At these words, Anat jumps up and grabs Joanna's hands, clinging to them tightly. Tears start down her face again, and her eyes are wide with fear. She sinks to her knees.

Joanna's anger melts away, and she pulls Anat into her arms. She strokes her hair and says, "I'm sorry, I'm sorry. It's just that I don't know what is going to happen to us." As Anat's sobs subside, the warmth of her small body soothes Joanna. After some moments, they go back to sewing. Joanna tries to smile and says, "Well, we will both do the best we can. We don't know what is going to happen, but we will figure it out. It's just that I am so scared." Anat smiles tentatively back, nodding in agreement, worry shadowing her eyes.

V

‒‒‒‒‒

Joanna straightens with a groan and lets her hoe fall. She brushes the dirt from her hands and then rubs them against her skirt. The skirt is barely cleaner than her hands. She looks down the row of barley, now ankle high. "My hands still ache," she thinks to herself, "and my back certainly does, but at least callouses have started to form."

The skin on their fingers no longer splits by the end of the day, as long as she remembers to massage their hands every night with oil. Getting up at daybreak is still hard to get used to, but at least now she can work longer without resting. Next to her Anat has stopped, too, flexing her fingers and taking a drink from the flask tied to her waist.

Two months have passed. Two months of farmwork: working from sunup to sundown with a break during the hottest part of the day. She and Anat are housed in a shed near the farmer's farthermost field. The farmer's wife delivers food and water to them every other day. She reports their progress to her husband, and sometimes he arrives himself to berate them for their apparent laziness. Twice a month, the farmer pays Joanna a pittance and gives Anat a small bag of grain instead of coins. Joanna's wages are usually accompanied by leers and suggestive remarks. She grimaces to herself. We won't be able to stay much longer, she thinks to herself. She is sure that fairly soon, the farmer will not be content with suggestive remarks. She and Anat need a kind of work which does not depend on the vagaries of weather or the whims of an overseer. But beggars can't be choosers, she reminds herself.

And Joanna is deeply lonely. With only a child for company, and a silent one at that, her feelings of fear and doubt cannot be expressed. She misses the company of women and her duties at the palace. She misses dreadfully using her skills as a midwife and being part of the happiness of families with their new babies. She still feels the shame of not being a cherished wife and anger at being rejected. It is hard to make plans when she feels so lost and abandoned. And she has stopped praying to the God who has allowed all this to happen. There is no comfort anywhere.

But that night, the way forward is decided for her. As she and Anat lie sleeping, the farmer silently enters the shed. He looms over Joanna, bends, and covers her mouth. His hand presses her down hard onto the pallet. She wakes startled and struggling. He starts fumbling with his clothes but then leaps back as Joanna slices his arm with the knife she has slept with since their arrival. She jumps up and backs the farmer into the open doorway. Joanna can hear her heart thumping, but she keeps brandishing the knife. They stare at one another until finally, the farmer turns and leaves, clutching his arm. Joanna stands at the doorway, looking over the moonlit field, afraid that he will come back. He disappears over the hill. As she turns to go inside, she can see that Anat is sitting bolt upright, her eyes wide in horror. Joanna embraces her. "Don't be afraid, Anat. Nothing really happened. We will leave now before daylight and make our way across country. We can find a better place to live, perhaps in one of the settlements by the Sea of Galilee. There are enough villages, especially on the southern end. We will stay well out of the way of Chuza's family in Capernaum."

Anat nods, crying a little.

"Besides, we are not cut out to be farmers anyway. I hate it, don't you?" Anat smiles a little and nods, and they both start packing up their belongings.

Two days later, they reach the end of the Valley of the Doves. Along the way, goldenrod and wildflowers have covered every crevice not cultivated for crops. But beyond the valley, nearer the water, terraced fields climb the small rises. And even closer to the water, the fields give way to small houses with attached sheds.

Most walls and fences are hung with cast nets. Small net weights are piled up against walls. Joanna decides to turn down the small road to Magdala, a fishing town she has often passed on her way to Capernaum but never visited. They can smell the water on the freshening air. Carts of fresh and salted fish rumble past them from the town to markets north and south. Joanna and Anat join the foot traffic going the other way, as local farmers and townspeople head into the market to select their own fish or to peddle produce, grains, and bread.

Joanna stops to speak to a woman seated by her front door mending a net. Her hands fly as she ties the loops and knots. The woman looks up without stopping her work and smiles. "It looks as if you have traveled a ways."

"Yes," agreed Joanna. "We have come from the fields west of Tiberius. We are looking for work and a place to stay. Do you have a need for a midwife here?"

The woman shakes her head. "No. We've had the same midwife for many years. She has been birthing babies here for a long time."

Pushing her disappointment to one side, Joanna asks, "Is there any other work here?"

"Can you mend nets?"

"No, but I could learn."

"Around here, most families mend and haul their own nets. But you should walk down to the shore and talk to Absalom, the tally master. He knows most of what needs doing around here, and he might be able to help you."

"I'm sorry to be ignorant, but what is a tally master?

The woman explains. "He supervises the teams of fishermen. He keeps everything fair. To find him, just keep along the road, past the synagogue, the marketplace, and the holding sheds. He will be easy to find near the shore."

"How will I recognize him?"

"Oh, that is easy. Absalom is usually the one shouting." She laughs at her own joke. Joanna thanks the woman and continues walking. The prosperity of the village is apparent in the sturdy stone synagogue and bustling marketplace. Soon they reach the shore.

It is midmorning, and fishermen are unloading their catches and throwing them into baskets. Some women quickly gut the fish, and another flurry of women are carrying the baskets over to the smoking area. Shallow charcoal trenches are lined with wooden tripods, and the fish are hung between them. The smell of fish guts, smoke, lake water, and sweat fills the air. Further down the beach, a team of men is pulling in a dragnet. The captured fish flounder and struggle, flashing silver. The sun glints off the water, and the small eddies and waves sparkle. A short, pugnacious-looking man with a weather-beaten face is gesturing and shouting as one end of the dragnet threatens to open up, losing the catch. He counts the fish and marks his tablet.

Joanna and Anat wait until the count is over. As the tally master trudges toward another group of fishermen, they follow him.

"Sir," Joanna says.

The master keeps trudging down the beach.

"Sir," she says again as she scoots around in front of him and stops.

"What? I am too busy to be hounded by strange women I don't know," he barks.

"A woman in the village says that you might be able to give us work or that you might know someone else who can."

The man takes a good look at them, noticing the stained and dusty clothes, the strain on their faces, the callouses on their hands.

But Joanna refuses to lower her eyes and faces him squarely. "I am trained as a midwife but will accept any kind of work."

"Where is your husband?"

"I have no husband."

Several moments pass as Absalom tries to stare her down, but she waits quietly. "Well, do you know how to sweep?" he finally says.

"Of course I do, and you would be getting two for the price of one."

He looks over at Anat. "Well, she's just a child, not to mention scrawny."

"She is a good worker and stronger than she looks."

"Well, we could use someone to clean the marketplace twice a day—once after midmorning and once after the stalls close for the evening. We could also use you to pick up after the women at noontime. They scoop up most of the fish parts after gutting, but someone still needs to come after them to pick up the scraps left behind. If we don't keep the beach clean, it becomes too slimy to walk." He turns to walk away.

Joanna stops him again. "And what would our pay be?"

He looks at her intently. "Do you have a place to stay?"

"Not yet."

"Well, how about the use of an old shed, a meal from the stalls at noon, and a bronze coin every month?"

Joanna grins broadly, and Anat smiles too. "That would be wonderful."

"Report tomorrow to Harmon at the marketplace. He runs the biggest stall. You can get your brooms and baskets there. And he will show you where to empty the garbage you collect. Just let him know that I sent you."

"Thank you, thank you."

"Yes, well, we'll see how well you do."

V I

The days that follow meld into a routine of sweeping, tidying around the stalls, picking up the beach, and returning to sweep the marketplace once again. With their main meal provided, much of the strain of day-to-day living is gone. For the most part, the vegetable vendors, as well as the fishmongers, are friendly, and there is always a bit of news or a joke going around. Joanna notices that Anat is beginning to relax and even to play when they return to their shed in the evening. The shed still has its roof, and there are several shelves along one wall. Originally, the shelves held fishing tackle, but now they hold their small collection of pots, lamps, and oils.

There is no place to cook inside, but Anat has dragged a tree limb over to their small charcoal firepit, so they have a place to sit as they cook. In her free time, she has collected a small mound of tiny snail shells and an even bigger mound of the small, colorful pebbles that make up the shoreline. Every night, she sorts through them, adding favorite ones she's collected during the day. She also has scavenged small bits of twine and rope and busies herself trying to make her own small net.

Settled, they now have time to wash their clothes and store their belongings. They even have time to sit staring at the embers of their small fires as they burn down. Joanna hopes that under Absalom's auspices, they won't be assaulted or robbed. But just in case, she buries most of the coins that were hidden in their skirts behind the shed in a little tin box. And just to be on the safe side, she still sleeps with her knife. She appreciates the protection the tally master's sponsorship has given her, but she doesn't want to take any chances.

While Anat has found interests to occupy her, Joanna finds the evenings difficult. With time to think, she still feels a deep loneliness, but her worries, which are not so great as they once were, can be tamped down. She tries not to think of her time as a wife, but when she does, feelings of shame and anger still overwhelm her. And the babies . . . how she misses the babies!

Some weeks later, Joanna and Anat have finished for the morning. Walking toward Harmon's stall to return the brooms, Joanna sees a finely dressed woman speaking to him. Her gold bracelets chime softly as she gestures. Her red hair blazes in the sun as her veil slips to one side. She adjusts it with a slim, white hand. She seems familiar, but Joanna can't remember where she has seen her. Too embarrassed to risk being recognized herself, Joanna pulls her veil further over her face. She starts to step away, but Harmon is already holding out his hand to take the brooms. The woman turns and looks at Joanna.

"I think I recognize you," the woman says. She pauses to think. "I know—the last time I saw you was at the house of Jairus in Capernaum. But what are you doing here in Magdala? And what are you doing working in the marketplace?"

Joanna stiffens, aware that her clothes are stained and smell of fish. They are a far cry from her former dress. "My name is Joanna, and I am from Tiberius. I was just visiting my brother-in-law—my ex-brother-in-law—when you saw me at the feast.

"Forgive my curiosity, but I still don't understand. This is a laborer's work. Surely your family does not approve."

Reluctantly, Joanna replies. "When I returned home from that visit, my husband cast me out. He had found a younger wife." Her face reddens with embarrassment. "We got work here cleaning the grounds and the shoreline."

Mary gestures toward Harmon. "I hope my steward has been kind to you. If not, I can speak to him. He can be a bit gruff." She grins at Harmon.

Joanna is so flustered she doesn't notice the smile. "No, please don't. He is quite nice, and I don't want to make him angry. We need this job."

"It's alright. He won't get mad. He drives a hard bargain with our customers, but it is all a big bluff."

"Besides," says Harmon, teasing back, "my lady, Mary, always gets what she wants—as long as she pays my wages on time."

Joanna looks back at Mary. "This business is yours?"

"Yes, and this is my steward. My husband died several years ago and left everything to me, since he had no family. Harmon keeps everything going smoothly."

"I'm sorry to hear about your husband."

"Thank you. I was fortunate. It was a good marriage. But here you see me in all my glory. I always get dressed up to come down here. People tend to want to buy from those who seem to be the most prosperous. I don't know why. I guess they think that my fish taste better." She laughs. She turns to Anat, who as usual is standing to one side, the leather bag hanging from her neck. "And who is this?" asks Mary.

"This is Anat. She is . . .was . . . my servant. We got thrown out together."

"Well, gather your faithful servant," Mary says grandly, teasing both of them. "My house is just down the road, and we can share the midday meal. I have someone I want you to meet—actually, a group of someones."

"Oh no, we couldn't! We are filthy and smell of fish." Joanna flushes with embarrassment.

"Then you will fit right in. They are a pretty unkempt bunch themselves. They travel a great deal throughout Galilee and Samaria and so are used to a little dust and fish guts. They follow Jesus, the rabbi who was at your brother-in-law's feast."

"No, we couldn't possibly . . ." stammers Joanna.

But Mary is already walking briskly, ushering Anat down the road. She turns and gestures to Joanna. "Come on, Joanna. Let's go. I'm hungry." Joanna finds herself following reluctantly.

After going down a side path, Mary swerves through an open gate in a long wall. Joanna stops hesitantly at the door. The courtyard is full of people. Joanna tries to make sense of all the activity swirling in the courtyard. Someone is grilling fish in the far corner under an ancient olive tree. A couple of men are taking bread from a small oven. Someone is filling cups with wine. An elderly woman is bustling from place to place, and there is a pregnant woman picking over a basket of dates with two small children. After a moment, Joanna recognizes her as the repentant woman at the feast. Several men lounge along the far wall, arguing about something or other.

Mary gestures for her to come in, and Joanna nods and washes her hands in the basin at the entrance and waits for Anat to finish. Mary takes them over to the man grilling the fish. He has his back to them and doesn't hear their approach.

Mary interrupts him. "Jesus, I have brought some visitors."

Startled, Jesus turns, accidentally burning his fingers on the grill. He grunts and puts his fingers in his mouth. "Mary, you scared me! Now you'll have to grill the fish." He groans. "I am far too injured to be able to do it!"

Mary laughs. "Alright, Jesus, I'll do your work for you. Anything to keep from hearing you complain."

Automatically, Joanna drops down beside Jesus and gestures for the medical bag around Anat's neck. Intent on her task, she forgets to be intimidated or worried about improprieties. She reaches for Jesus' hand and examines the burns. Mary finishes the cooking of the fish as Joanna sees to his fingers. She takes some salve from her bag and slathers it over the burns. As she looks over the fingers, she says, "Only one will need a small bandage. Not too much damage has been done."

As she prepares the small strip of linen, Jesus says, "I recognize you. You were in Capernaum at Jairus's house."

Joanna is surprised that he remembers her. "Yes, I was there. It was my brother-in-law's house."

"Was?"

"Yes . . . and no. I mean, it still is his house but I am no longer his sister-in-law." She feels her face redden and waits for censure or probing questions, but Jesus is silent, and when she looks up at him, his brown eyes are friendly and warm.

Despite a familiar rush of shame, Joanna feels impelled to tell Jesus the truth about her situation. "I was married to his brother, Chuza. He is Herod Agrippa's steward in Tiberius. I spent my married life going between the palaces in Tiberius and Jerusalem and the port city of Jaffa, depending on the time of year and the caravan schedules. And we often visited his brother and mother in Capernaum."

"How long were you married?

"Four years." Bitterness colors her words. "He divorced me because I could not have children. My mother and father trained me as a midwife, but since I now have no community, I work here cleaning the marketplace."

As usual, Anat had remained close at hand, following the conversation intently.

"And yet, here you are with a child," said Jesus, laying a hand lightly on Anat's arm.

Unable to help herself, Joanna blurts, "But she is not my child. She is just a . . ."

"Just a what?" Jesus' question has a hint of a challenge to it.

"She is just . . . Anat is nine. She has been my servant since she was five. Chuza bought her and gave her to me as a gift when we were married. She is mute. She has never talked."

The small bandaging is finished. Joanna hands the salve and linen back to Anat, who puts them away. Joanna starts to stand up as Jesus reaches out for her to stay. She sinks back down as Jesus continues speaking. "I assume that you didn't steal her from your former home."

"Oh, no. Chuza said I could take her." She grimaces. "Or rather, he said I could take whatever I could carry, so I picked her up. I don't know exactly why. I wasn't thinking straight."

Anat hears this, and her eyes indicate how hurt she is. She backs away and goes to sit by herself.

Silence falls. Jesus looks thoughtfully at Anat and then turns back. "Tell me, Joanna—you say you don't know why you picked her up. Are you sure?"

The question penetrates Joanna's heart, and she is stricken. Thoughts fly through her mind, fueled by anger and fear. Her emotions rise up, and she can't keep quiet at the implied criticism. She spits out a torrent of words aimed straight at him. "I need a home. I need money. I need Chuza to regret what he has done! I need for my life to go back to the way it was. I don't need someone else's child. How can I take care of a child? Any child?" The silence returns. Joanna can hear her own breath, rapid and shallow.

Finally, Jesus responds, his voice low. "Doesn't the psalmist say, 'When I am afraid, I will trust in you? In God, whose word I praise, in God I trust; I will not be afraid'? In faith, don't we ask, 'What can mortal man do to me?'" Joanna is struck by the intensity of his gaze. "Generations have had hard lives, difficult lives, but the LORD is faithful and is always with us."

Hearing these words spoken with such clarity and sincerity, Joanna's feels her anger leaching away, exposing her loneliness and despair. "I used to believe that. But what can mortal man do to me? He can do whatever he wants. Obviously, the psalmist wasn't a woman like me. God doesn't care. I am barren and tossed aside."

Jesus and Joanna look intently at each other. Suddenly, Jesus waggles his bandaged finger. Joanna can't help but smile at this small joke.

"And yet, here you are—a skilled healer. We shall feed you breakfast in thanksgiving for your help." He calls out to one of the men. "Judas—bring some bread here for our guests."

A man approaches and begrudgingly gives Joanna some bread. Jesus indicates that he take some to Anat also. Barely audible, the man mutters, "Just what we need—two more mouths to feed." Jesus holds his hand up in slight rebuke, and he turns away.

"Don't mind him," Jesus says, laughing. "His name is Judas, and he is the keeper of the purse and is always worried that our little collection of coins will run out and we no longer will be able to feast like we are this morning."

Mary Magdalene approaches. "But luckily, we have stalwart friends who always make sure we have plenty of fish." Mary laughs and leads Joanna and Anat over to the small group of women and children, where they share a meal of grilled fish, bread, and dates. She introduces Susanna, her children, and Nahash, the mother of two of the men. After the meal, Mary introduces Joanna and Anat to the other followers of Jesus, and Joanna is struck by how different the men all are. Some are well- spoken; some are taciturn; some seem educated; most are not—but all are pleasant and greet her politely.

Later, Joanna and Anat are standing by the gate, ready to go back to their work in the marketplace. "Thank you for the meal, Mary." She looks around, bemused and confused. "If you don't mind me saying so, I think this is the oddest group of people I have ever met, and Jesus isn't anything like the rabbis I am used to."

Mary grins. "We are an unusual group, I know. It is hard to make sense of it if you don't know our stories. But why don't you come to dinner at sundown tomorrow night? Jesus and the men will be gone. They usually visit the fishermen after their day's work on the lake is finished. Perhaps that will give us a chance to talk. Susanna and I can tell you how we came to be at Jairius's house that night."

V I I

The next evening, the women and children are washing the dishes after the meal. The children chatter sleepily as the half-moon rises.

Nahash groans softly as she stands up and announces, "I am going to go to bed. My old bones are tired. I will take the dishes in, and I might as well take the little ones too." She trundles grumpily into the house with the two children in tow.

Susanna smiles. "All this travel around Galilee is hard on Nahash, but she won't let her sons out of her sight! She thinks they can't get along without her, but I think they have finally persuaded her to go home to Capernaum. James and John are very patient with her."

Mary nods in agreement. The three women arrange themselves comfortably near the cooking fire. Anat curls up nearby in her cloak and soon falls asleep.

"Do you all travel together often?" asks Joanna.

"It depends on where Jesus is going. His ministry takes him all over, sometimes even to Judea and Samaria. For the last few months, Susanna and her children have gone with them, along with Nahash, of course. I usually stay here to provide a base for everyone and to make enough money for them to use on their travels."

Susanna rubs her belly and sighs. "It is getting close to my time. As much as I would like to, I can't continue to travel, and my other two need a stable home. Jesus has helped me believe that I can have a proper future. But it will be difficult." She lapses into silence.

Joanna looks at the coals and at the firelight flickering over the faces of Mary, Susanna, and Anat's sleeping figure. Somehow, she no longer feels so curious about how all these people came together. For the moment, it is enough to be in the company of women. She casts a practiced eye over Susanna. Two or three more weeks to go, probably, she thinks. I wish her well.

Susanna's voice interrupts her thoughts. "You are probably wanting to know why I was at your brother-in-law's house."

Joanna reassures her, "Only if you want to tell me. I don't really need to know."

Susanna pauses and then says, "I want to tell you. God has blessed me, and I want to give him praise and acknowledge the honor he has bestowed on me." She continues, "I have been a prostitute for a long time—the reasons don't really matter except that I didn't have a choice." She doesn't notice that Joanna has stiffened in reaction to how naturally Susanna speaks of the unspeakable. "I lived in a hut outside Capernaum with first one baby and then two. The righteous would visit me under the cover of darkness, and the unrighteous would arrive at any hour. Everyone nearby knew this, of course, and knew that my children had no father. I was the town scandal. I think every town has to have one; otherwise, what would everyone gossip about?" She grimaces. "I often would fantasize about starting another life somewhere else. I had even saved some money, but I never had enough. Every day, I would awake to shame and anger. I hated who I was, and I hated the men even more."

Susanna pauses. Joanna wants to say some words of comfort, but nothing seems adequate. Susanna continues, "But most of all, I hated the women in my neighborhood. They would never let my children play with theirs and would always turn away at the well or at the town ovens. They were so smug and self-righteous. They would narrow their eyes whenever they saw me and whisper about me endlessly. I longed to tell them exactly whose husbands visited me. Exactly whose husbands handed me a pittance. Exactly whose husbands pretended to be God-fearing. This anger and hate were so strong in me they rose like bile. I could feel it sear my throat.

"But one day about five months ago, I was in the marketplace in Capernaum right before sundown buying food. My pregnancy barely showed yet, and I was hoping that no one would notice that I was again with child. Suddenly, a crowd came out of nowhere, and in the middle of all the people were Jesus and his disciples. Mary was there, too, with some other women, though I didn't know who they were then. There was a lot of noise and jostling, so I stepped to one side to get out of the way. I asked the person next to me what was happening.

"'It's Jesus,' she said over the din, 'the prophet and teacher. The crowd has followed him in from the countryside.'

"Just then, Jesus lifted his hand and the crowd quieted. And he began to speak. His voice was low and firm and rolled out over the crowd. 'Who is like our God, who removes guilt and pardons sin for the remnant of his inheritance? It is for us, it is for each one of you—for his people Israel. And who is like our Father, who does not persist in anger but delights in clemency?'

"Jesus continued. 'If you forgive others their transgressions, our heavenly Father will forgive you. But if you do not forgive others, neither will your Father forgive your sins. As you treat others, so will you be treated. He will brush away your offenses like a cloud, your sins like a mist; return to our Father. Again I say, return to our Father. He wants his children to turn to him. He offers you redemption.'

"When Jesus finished and turned to continue down the road, he looked straight at me. I will never forget that look. I started to cry. Jesus motioned to Mary and pointed at me, and she started walking toward me. Embarrassed, I hurried away with tears still falling. Over the next several days, Jesus' words echoed in my head. I thought about how much my shame and anger had harmed me and harmed my children too. Anger had ruled my life for so long. Was it possible to forgive all that had happened, knowing how cruel and hypocritical people were? I knew that Jesus was still in the area, but I was afraid to approach him. He was always in the midst of people, many of whom knew me. I was sure they would tell him about me and he would send me away."

Joanna looks at Susanna with sympathy as Mary takes Susanna's hand.

Seeing that Joanna is not condemning her, she clutches Mary's hand and continues. "Early one morning, I was at the well, and Mary was there too. We began talking. As we drew water, I admitted that I had run away from her. Later, she accompanied me home and met my children, and I told her my story. Over the next several days, we met and talked several times. She accepted me, despite my livelihood. She helped me plan how my life might be able to change with some help. But she also said that repentance and sorrow for my own sins needed to come first. By this time, I longed to unburden myself and asked Mary to help me. As a sign of my intent, I spent most of my money on a flask of fragrant oils, and you know the rest." Susanna's voice dwindles in the night air.

"Since then, Susanna and her children have stayed with us until we are able to find them a permanent home," adds Mary.

After a moment, Susanna says, "Well, after that long story, I think it is time I went to bed too. I probably told you more than you wanted to know. I hope you weren't too shocked. Good night."

"Good night, and thank you. I think you are very brave," said Joanna.

"No, not really," sighs Susanna. "Just desperate. But my heart is so much lighter now. My spirit is renewed. The anger still rises, but more and more I am able to forgive those who have hurt me."

Mary and Joanna sit together in silence as Susanna walks inside. Joanna ponders Susanna's story. She tries to reconcile what she is hearing with the religious teachings that have been a part of her life. According to those teachings, a holy man like Jesus should shun women, especially women like Susanna. Joanna says, "But I still don't understand. How can you all be living and traveling with one another? You aren't related. Surely you face criticism and condemnation in the places that you visit?"

"Yes, it is true that sometimes the criticism is severe and the rejection is immediate. But Jesus has his own way. It is Jesus who has called each one of us to his service. We have kinship through our relationship with him. We trust him, and we trust those he trusts. We all have had different experiences. Some of the men were fishermen and were disciples of John the Baptist. I was healed by Jesus. Some men were called from their places of business. We are very different from one another, but we all believe in Jesus and that he has the words of eternal life. I and other women minister to him and the disciples in order to allow them to spread his message. We contribute money and goods. We try to help. We don't always travel with Jesus, but sometimes we do!"

"I just have a hard time imagining such a life."

"Is it so different really? Our ancestors traveled together in the wilderness for forty years. Rabbis have always had their followers. For us, being near Jesus is more important than anything. More important than hardship, more important than criticism. We have so much to learn about our heavenly Father, things only Jesus knows."

"You must be convinced of the truth of Jesus' teachings to have such faith in him."

"I am. We all are."

"So how do you cope with the harassment?"

"Most of the time, we don't need to cope with it. We travel as a group, and they don't call James and John the 'sons of thunder' for nothing!" Mary Magdalene laughs, and Joanna laughs with her.

"It is not so much the harassment and shunning but the religious hostility. Many, especially Pharisees, object to Jesus' message of love and tolerance. You saw that yourself at your brother-in-law's. The bigger Jesus' crowds become, the angrier the Pharisees become. There are sometimes ferocious condemnations. But not all the time. Many ordinary people are receptive." Both women stare at the embers in the fire as silence falls, then Mary stands. "But come, it's quite late. It's time to go to bed for us too."

They rise, and Joanna shakes Anat awake. She gets up, and they both pass through the front gate. A shooting star streaks unobserved overhead. At the shed, Anat falls asleep almost immediately, but long into the early morning Joanna thinks about all that she has heard.

A week goes by. Joanna and Anat work diligently at their tasks. Both are beginning to be accepted by the fishermen and their families. The vendors in the marketplace like Joanna, for the most part, and chat with Anat, even though she never answers. Unused to this kind of life, Joanna is impressed with how closely the families work together—the men fishing, the women drying the fish, the younger sons taking dried and fresh fish to sell to inland villages, and the girls preparing meals and mending nets. Their family bonds are strong, and Joanna envies their care of one another. Several times, Joanna and Anat are invited to share a meal at Mary's house. Jesus and his disciples go back and forth between Magda and the other southern lake villages, and Joanna gets to know some of the men a little.

The fishermen of the group have an easy comradery. It is easy to tell that Simon Peter and his brother Andrew, and James and his brother John, have worked with one another. They all have the stocky builds and the broad shoulders of net haulers. Sometimes when they walk, they even seem to roll, as if they are still standing on a boat. They are boisterous and like to joke and shove one another when discussions get intense. The others are harder to get to know. Judas especially is prickly and often exchanges small complaints with Nahash about others in the group. John, who is younger than the rest, is quieter and more introspective when he is not with his brother. He usually stays close to Jesus and is a man of few words. James and Philip are curious and often ask her questions about midwifery. A few of the disciples are Zealots, but the others seem to have no interest in politics whatsoever. Gradually, Joanna becomes aware that Simon Peter is their leader. The others listen when he makes a request or an observation, and it is he who organizes their daily activities.

But it is Jesus Joanna watches most closely, hoping to understand what the others see in him. Here at Mary's house in Magdala, he is relaxed and enjoys playing with Susanna's children. He usually takes charge of whatever in a pot needs stirring, and he chats comfortably during dinner conversations. He delights in Mary's sense of humor, especially when she pokes fun at the silliness of everyday life. His laugh is infectious, and it doesn't take much to get the whole group smiling and laughing.

Joanna wishes she could be there in the mornings, since the group spends them in instruction and prayer, but she is always working. She envies Mary, who can sometimes leave her tasks to her steward and sit and listen. Susanna attends, too, listening carefully, usually with a pile of mending in her lap. If only she had the leisure to hear and absorb Jesus' teachings, maybe she would understand more.

After dinner, Jesus usually tells a story. The stories often perplex Joanna. He speaks of a widow, or a rich man, or a dishonest steward. The stories aren't like the ones that end with a moral. They are simple but not obvious; and there is always a twist to them. But she doesn't feel the attraction that Susanna or the crowds that follow him seem to have. On the contrary, when he is not teaching or participating in the preparation of a meal, he carries that deep silence wrapped around him like a blanket. It puzzles and scares her a little. Sometimes when spoken to, he startles a bit, as if his thoughts have been far away. And she notices that usually before she and Anat go back to their little house each night, Jesus slips away to walk the beach by himself.

One evening, Joanna and Anat come at dinner time, but the men have gone fishing that afternoon and haven't returned. While they wait for them to come back, the women idly talk. Susanna especially is full of questions about life in the palace. After Joanna answers some of the questions as best she can, Mary asks, "Joanna, how did you come to marry Chuza? Where did you meet him?"

"I met Chuza in Jaffa. It was his first time coming to the harbor as Herod's steward in Tiberius, and he was overseeing the unloading of goods from an Egyptian ship onto the camels. One of his men had been injured by some falling crates, and they brought him to my father's house to be treated. My father was a well-known doctor in the area. We met then because my mother and I assisted my father with the cleaning and bandaging of the wounds. My parents were pleased that he showed interest in me and encouraged him to return the next day. So that's how we met . . ." Joanna's voice trails off.

"My parents were very devout Jews and were careful to fulfill all of the righteous practices," she remembers with a smile, "but they disagreed about almost everything else. They had the most amazing arguments, which would end with my mother giggling and my father trying hard not to chuckle. I was an only child, and we had a very comfortable life with my father's work as a doctor and my mother's vocation as a midwife. When I turned ten, I would go with my mother to assist. That's how I learned to help women in labor.

"Anyway, the next day when Chuza came back, he met with my father and asked about my bride price. The amount was agreeable to him. As for my parents, they were impressed with his connection to the palace and wanted nothing more than to secure a prosperous husband for me and security for the children we would have. Chuza returned to Tiberius overseeing the caravan, and for several months he sent me messages every couple of weeks with merchants that were traveling to the harbor. When he returned to Jaffa, we were married. He took me back to Tiberius, and we had a sizable house just down the road from the palace construction site. Two years ago, the palace was finished, and we moved into a large apartment off the main courtyard. Since Chuza went back and forth to the Jaffa harbor three or four times a year, my parents and I were happy that we would be able to see so much of each other. But three months after my wedding, my parents were stricken with fever. I left as soon as I received word, but they died before I had traveled even halfway back."

Joanna continues almost as if she is talking to herself. "I used to be proud that Chuza and I never argued, that we were always civil with one another. But maybe it really meant that he did not care enough for me to bother with arguing or even talking. We generally went our own separate ways during the daytime, and as long as I didn't let my work as a midwife interfere with my wifely duties, all remained serene. But babies often come in the middle of the night and at inconvenient times. We argued about it more and more. I must have been blind. I never dreamed that Chuza would abandon me." Joanna looks wistfully at Susanna's swollen belly. "I don't know why God wouldn't give us children."

VIII

—

One afternoon, Mary approaches Joanna as she finishes work for the day. "Peace, Joanna! May I walk with you?"

"Certainly."

Joanna and Anat hand in their brooms, and all three stroll down to the beach. Anat drifts off in search of interesting shells.

"Joanna, Jesus has a request of you," Mary begins.

"For me?"

"Do you remember when I told you that all of us had been called to follow Jesus?"

"Yes, of course I do."

"Well, you might say that Jesus is calling you, or rather, he is asking a favor of you."

Joanna looks at Mary in surprise.

Mary continues on. "You know Susanna is near her time."

"Of course, and I am certainly willing to attend her if she wishes it."

"Yes, Susanna told me, and that is good of you, but, well, it is a little complicated. In several days, Jesus and his disciples will be traveling back to Capernaum and then on to Bethsaida. Simon Peter's mother, who lives in Capernaum, knows of two widows who have a small farm on a hillside outside of Bethsaida. They are in need of more hands and young backs to help them. They are willing to take in Susanna and her family. No one there will know of Susanna's past, and she will be able to start again. But we are worried, since her time is so near. Could you go with her in case a midwife is needed? I will be staying here in order to . . ."

Startled, anxiety starts to seize Joanna, and she vehemently shakes her head no, as if to trying to stop the words.

"... make arrangements for the journey down to Jerusalem for Passover. Nahash will be going north too. James and John have persuaded her to go back home. They don't want her to make the long trek to Jerusalem. All of you, except for Nahash and Susanna, should be back in about two weeks."

Joanna still shakes her head no. "But I'm not a disciple. I am not part of your group. I barely know any of you, and what about my work here? I can't just get up and leave. I don't want to lose my job. And what do I do about Anat? It's a crazy idea!"

Mary nods her head but continues anyway, taking Joanna's hands. "Now, listen. I know that you and Anat cannot be separated, but if Anat goes with you she can help with the two younger children. She is very good with them. And as for your job here, I can make sure that Absalom doesn't give your job away to anyone else. And this is a perfect chance to hear more of Jesus' teaching. Didn't you tell me that you wish you could hear more?"

Joanna is shaken and bewildered. The security that she has felt since coming to Magdala—her job, the routine, the companionship—all are being snatched away. She owes Mary a great deal, but does that mean she has to start following Jesus around in order to pay Mary back for befriending her?

Mary continues with her next argument. "And surely you have a responsibility to Susanna? You are a midwife. It is what you are meant to do. You don't want her to give birth by the side of the road surrounded by a bunch of Galilean fishermen, do you?

Joanna says, "No, I suppose not. That would be horrible." She glances at Mary, who is looking at her tenderly. Joanna wonders if Mary is imagining, like she is, Peter and James bent over a laboring woman. "No, actually that would be quite horrible." They both burst into gales of laughter. Joanna pulls Anat into her embrace. "Anat, what do you think? Should we help Susanna?" Anat nods and pats the ever-present bag. "Alright, Mary, you convinced us. We'll go." Joanna smiles ruefully, and Anat gives a little skip of excitement.

The next morning finds them on the road heading toward Capernaum and Bethsaida along the Sea of Galilee. The women, children, and disciples are spread out. Joanna is walking with Susanna, and Anat is holding hands with Susanna's two children. Suddenly, Nahash pushes by them and snags James as she goes by. She drags him with her up to Jesus, who is walking ahead with John. Jesus stops as Nahash draws near. Her sons shuffle nervously, obviously embarrassed by their mother's action. Everyone gathers around in order hear. Jesus' face turns solemn, as if he knows what is going to happen next.

"What do you want of me, woman?" he asks. Joanna has never heard this tone in his voice before.

Nahash, seeing Jesus' expression, hesitates for a moment and then blurts out, "Lord, please say that my two sons may sit, one on your right hand, and the other on your left, when you come into your kingdom." James and John squirm uncomfortably when they hear what their mother is asking. She is speaking loudly enough so that all can hear. The other disciples are irritated by her words, and some are even angry, muttering to themselves. Even though she notices the negative reaction, pride and stubbornness prompt her to continue. "They are good boys, true and faithful, and they have done everything you have asked of them."

"Nahash, you have a mother's heart, but you do not know what you are asking." Jesus turns to James and John. His face becomes even more grave. "And what do you two say? Do you want what your mother is asking? Can you drink the chalice I shall drink, no matter how bitter?"

They say, "we can."

Jesus turns around, staring at the rest of the disciples. They shift their feet uneasily. Joanna is glad that this stare is not directed at her. "And what about the rest of you? Can you drink from the chalice I will drink?"

"Yes."

"I can."

"We will."

"It is true that indeed you shall drink from my chalice, although you do not understand what you are saying; but to sit on my right or left hand is not mine to give to you, but to them for whom it is prepared by my Father!"

The disciples accept the rebuke and look at one another, aware that they have let Jesus down. Nahash scuttles back to the other women.

As they continue walking, Joanna murmurs to Susanna, "It's as if Jesus believes that the LORD is his father. As if the LORD is his actual father!"

Susanna nods. "We believe; we hope . . ."

Joanna doesn't know what to say in response, so she stays quiet.

It's noon on the second day of their journey. They are about five miles outside of Capernaum. The stunted trees next to the road are aromatic but provide little shade. The heat presses down hard, and most are tired. The disciples are grumpily eating, and Susanna's children are pestering one another. Jesus has gone over and sat down under a large bush shading some boulders. Nahash is already napping, her head cushioned on her cloak. Joanna unpacks a small container of food for Anat and then goes over to Susanna to check on her. She is eating listlessly and shifts often, trying to find a comfortable sitting position. "Are you having any pain?" Joanna asks.

"No, but my feet are making it difficult to walk." She holds up one puffy, red foot. Her ankle has swollen to almost twice its normal size. Joanna motions to Anat for her bag. She leads Susanna to a different spot so that her face is in the shade. She puts a flat bundle under her head and a smaller one under the small of her back and rolls up a large cloak to prop up her feet. Picking out a jar of ointment, she starts to massage Susanna's feet, stroking firmly upward first from toe to ankle, then foot to knee.

"Oh, that feels so good!" gasps Susanna. "Thank you, thank you."

By the time Joanna is finished massaging her other foot, Susanna is fast asleep.

Joanna gets up and sees that the children have followed Jesus and are pulling on his arms, clambering in his lap, and chattering away.

"Come away, children. Jesus needs a little peace and quiet. Let's play a game over here before your nap."

"It's alright. Let them come to me; do not prevent them, for after all, the kingdom of God belongs to such as these." Jesus laughs and tickles them. "They are quite good company. Sit down, Joanna. You need to rest also."

The disciples approach a minute later. Simon Peter says, "Jesus, we are so close to my mother's home. Let some of us continue on and prepare for when the rest of you arrive."

James says, "John and I will stay here with our mother and the other women."

Jesus looks over at Nahash and Susanna, who are still asleep. "Yes, that's a good idea. We will see the rest of you later this afternoon."

As they leave, Jesus turns back to the children. "Let's all play a game together." James and John quickly back away and go to sit by their sleeping mother. Jesus laughs at their obvious reluctance to join in the game. Joanna, Anat, and the children hunker down in front of him.

"So, children, what does the chicken say?"

"Bok, bok, bok," they respond.

"What does the goat say?"

"Maa, maa, maa."

"What does the dog say?"

"Woof, woof."

The younger children are all smiles, but all the while Jesus is playing the game, he glances from time to time at Anat, who is solemnly listening. It is clear from the expression on her face that she wants to participate but can't. "Well, before your naps we can have a story. I think the story should be about . . . it is about a little lamb."

He begins, "There once was a shepherd who had a hundred sheep. That's this many!" Jesus stretches his arms wide. The children laugh. "And one day he saw that the littlest lamb was missing. Her mother was crying for her and looking everywhere, but the lamb wasn't with the rest of the flock. So the shepherd got his cloak and his staff and started looking. He looked in the bushes, he looked up the side of the hill, he looked on the other side of the hill, he looked in the rocks. He looked everywhere, but he couldn't find the lamb. Suddenly, he heard a little cry and saw a tiny bit of white. The lamb was caught on a thornbush deep in a gully, and she was very frightened. Carefully, the shepherd climbed down the steep, rocky hill. He freed her from the thorns, put her over his shoulders, and carried her up back up the hill to her mother. The lamb immediately started suckling because she was so hungry! Seeing this, the shepherd rejoiced and was very glad." The children smile at the happy ending, and Jesus looks over at Joanna as he continues. "I tell you, in just the same way, there will be more joy in heaven over one sinner who repents then over ninety-nine righteous people who have no need of repentance."

"Now you two go lay down." He shoos the two smaller children over to their mother, and they curl up next to her. He looks at Anat. Jesus gestures towards her, and she goes up to him and leans into his side. Jesus puts his arm around her and holds her close. Joanna is amazed when she sees that that Anat is crying. Anat never cries!

Jesus murmurs, "Anat, don't cry. The lamb is safe with her mother. The shepherd will keep them close and safe." Jesus strokes her hair, and she quiets. Gently, Jesus lifts one hand and places the tips of his fingers lightly over her mouth, still wet with her tears. Then he places his other hand on her head. Anat closes her eyes. It is so quiet that Joanna can hear the insects thrumming and Jesus' breathing.

After several moments, Jesus removes his hands and says, "Anat, little one, what does the lamb say?"

"Baa, baa," comes the answer so softly that Joanna is not quite sure she has heard it at all. Transfixed, she stares at Anat, her breath caught in her throat.

Jesus continues. "And what does the cat say?"

"Meow, meow, *meow!*"

The three of them look at one another and grin.

"And what does Joanna say?"

Anat says, "Anat, Anat, come here!" Her voice is thin and tinny, with a Coptic accent, but it is a voice.

Joanna starts to laugh and cry at the same time. Jesus laughs, too, as Joanna sweeps Anat up in her arms.

That night in the courtyard of the house of Peter's mother, Miriam, all are bedded down next to the banked fire, the men on one side, the women on the other. James and John have left to take their mother home and plan to stay overnight. When the travelers had arrived earlier, there was quiet jubilation and surprise over Anat's healing, and the disciples teased her about her raspy voice. Miriam gave her warm milk with honey to drink to soothe her throat, and John teased her about her accent. It was clear from her speech that Anat was from Egypt and that some of the Aramaic words and sounds were difficult for her.

As Joanna lay looking at the stars, she found that she was disconcerted by Anat's newfound voice. She was used to thinking of Anat as a silent servant, biddable, almost without personality. When she couldn't talk, Joanna found that she was easy to ignore. Now that she could talk, what was Anat really like? And what was she thinking about all that had happened to her?

Joanna turns her head and sees that Anat has not fallen asleep yet. She picks up her blanket and lays down closer to her and whispers, "Anat—do you remember your life before we brought you to the palace? Do you remember the day you were sold?"

The answer comes in a whisper: "Yes."

"Do you remember anything else?"

"Yes."

"Please tell me what you remember."

"I remember my mother. She had warm hands, but she cried a lot. I had a brown puppy. But then there was a bad man and a lot of noise. He is the one who took me. I cried for my mother, but he wouldn't let me go back home. He said that if I kept crying, he would kick my puppy; and he said that if I told anyone anything, he would kick my mother too."

"So you were quiet."

"I needed to be very quiet."

"Do you remember the trip to Jaffa?"

"Yes. There was a lady who helped me sometimes, but she got sick. It was a long, long way. There was a very big man who had a black beard. He put ropes on you if you tried to run away. But I was good. I never said anything. And I never ran away."

Joanna has a hard time controlling her tears as she thinks about how terrorized Anat had been.

"Anat, do you remember the name your mother gave you?"

"Yes, my name was Rina."

"Rina is a beautiful name. Would it be alright if I called you that? I would like to call you by the name your mother gave you."

Anat doesn't say anything. Joanna rolls over on her mat to face her and takes her hand. "I'm so sorry, Rina. I'm sorry for everything. I wish that I could give you back to your mother, but we will never be able to find her after all this time. I know that our life now is hard, and I know that I haven't always been kind. I have taken you for granted and not thought about what you might need or want." She struggles to find the right words. She is chastened thinking of how she treated Rina like a slave—ordering her about, taking advantage of her, molding her into the perfect little assistant. How kind had she been to that little five-year-old who had been sold and carted away to a harbor town far away from her mother?

"But I wonder how you would feel—well, how would you feel about changing things? We could decide to be a family; we could choose to be mother and daughter just like Jesus and his friends have decided to be family. I could be the mother and you could be the daughter. You wouldn't be a servant anymore."

There was a long silence. Finally, Rina says, "For always?"

"Always. I promise."

"But what if you can't take care of me? What if we run out of food? Will you sell me?"

Joanna's heart breaks a little at these questions. She is ashamed that Rina remembers her cruel words of before. "I promise I will take care of you. We will share everything. If we have nothing, we will share nothing. If I have something, you will get half. I can even teach you more about being a midwife, if you want. You are very smart and very patient. I know you would do well."

More silence. "Can I still carry the bag?"

"Yes, Rina, you can carry the bag." There is a smile in Joanna's voice. "But you must tell me if it gets too heavy." Joanna can hear that Rina has started crying. She pulls her in close and clutches her tight. "I'm sorry, Rina. I love you, and I'm so sorry for all the ways I have hurt you. But shall we be a family? What do you say? Shall you be Rina, daughter of Joanna? I would be so proud if you would say yes."

Softly, Rina says, "Baa, baa."

They both start to laugh and cry at the same time. Rina falls asleep almost immediately, worn out by the tumult of the day, but Joanna remains wide awake, cradling her close and weeping silently, thinking about Jesus, and the healing, and how life has changed once again.

I X

Two days later, after a leisurely breakfast in Capernaum, Joanna accompanies Susanna, her children, and Jesus to a small holding in the hills outside Bethsaida. The three-hour walk is an easy one along a northern track away from the water. The farm is the home of Sophie and Evit, the two sisters who are offering a home to Susanna and her children. The house is plain and simple but well cared for. Next to the house is a lean-to sheltering grinding stones of varying sizes and baskets of grain and flour. Several sheep mill about in a small pen nearby, munching hay from a trough under a wide roof. A newly plowed field spreads out behind. Stooping out through the small door, the two women come to greet them. Their faces wreathed with smiles, they beam at Jesus and welcome the others. They ask everyone inside to be seated out of the sun and fetch a light lunch, plus small honey cakes for the children.

Not put off in the least by Susanna's condition or her rather tense and worried face, Sophie and Evit talk about their plans for their small mill and other projects they can start with Susanna to help them. They take Susanna and Jesus on a brief tour of their four big rooms and show her the one set aside for her and the children. A basket of swaddling clothes is placed next to the bed, and a tiny window lets in some light.

Jesus laughs and teases Susanna: "Well, it certainly seems as if you are going to be very busy. I hope you can handle all this and a new baby, too."

Evit objects, "My sister and I will help. The baby to come and the children here now are such a blessing for old women such as ourselves."

"I'm going to teach them how to take care of the sheep," says Sophie. "And maybe we will even get a goat."

The children nod enthusiastically, and all the adults chuckle. After they finish the short tour, Jesus draws Susanna aside to confer.

Joanna walks out into the yard with the two women to give Jesus and Susanna more privacy. She thanks the sisters for their generosity in adopting Susanna and her children. They demur and ask about Susanna's condition.

"She is quite near her time," says Joanna, "but the pains have not started yet. Here is a small bottle of hyssop in case the labor becomes too intense. Here, too, is some salve and more fresh linens, even though it is obvious you are well prepared. It is her third birth and should go quite easily, God willing."

The women collect Susanna and the children's belongings and Joanna's supplies and take them into the house. When Susanna comes out, her face is relaxed, but her eyes are misting. The time for parting has come.

The women come out and put their arms around Susanna and her children, and the oldest sister asks Jesus for a blessing. The small group quiets.

Jesus extends his arms and looks to heaven. "Blessed are you, oh Lord, our God, King of the universe, who have allowed us to live, have preserved us, and have enabled us to reach this season. Protect what your right hand has planted. Grant these women peace and long life, and may they give glory to your name."

Holding back her tears, Joanna embraces Susanna and kisses her, murmuring her own small blessing. Then Jesus, Rina, and Joanna turn to go. When they reach the track again, Joanna turns and sees that Susanna is waving. She waves back with a sorrowful heart, but with hope and optimism that this will be a peaceful and safe place for Susanna and her children.

The next day back in Capernaum, Joanna and Rina are beginning to trudge up a hill outside the town. On either side of them, as far as they can see, people are sitting in ones, twos, and in family groups. It is mostly a crowd of the ragged and the poor, with small clumps of townspeople, community leaders, and Pharisees interspersed among them. Joanna keeps an eye out for Jairus but doesn't see him. She doesn't know if she wants to talk to him or if she would rather avoid him altogether. The hillside is steep, and the sun is beating down. Many of the children they pass are fretful. There is weariness on the faces of the adults, but they are still listening. Jesus is standing at the top of the hill. His voice is strong, and as usual, it rolls and flows over the crowd.

Suddenly, there is a loud wail to their right and down the hill a ways. Joanna sees a toddler whose head is covered in blood. His mother tries to staunch the blood with a cloth, but she can't tend the wound and hold the flailing child at the same time. Joanna and Rina hurry down to help.

"We can help you. I am a midwife," Joanna says reassuringly. Rina pulls out clean linens from the bag, and Joanna presses the edges of the gash together. "The cut is deep," Joanna tells the mother. "We will need to sew it up . . . just two or three stitches. Do you have anything that might distract your child while we work?" The mother offers a pitted date for the baby to suck on, and soon the cries turn into little whimpers. Joanna works swiftly with Rina's help. When the small crisis is over, the mother thanks Joanna profusely.

As Joanna stands, she can hear that Jesus is still speaking. "But to you who hear what I say, love your enemies, do good to those who hate you, bless those who curse you, pray for those who mistreat you. To the person who strikes you on one cheek, offer the other one as well, and from the person who takes your cloak, do not withhold even your tunic. Do to others as you would have others do unto you. For if you love those who love you, what credit is that to you? Even sinners love those who love them.

But rather, love your enemies and do good to them, and lend expecting nothing back; then your reward will be great and you will be children of the Most High, for he himself is kind to the ungrateful and the wicked. Be merciful, just as your Father is merciful."

Two-thirds of the way up the hill, Joanna reaches Judas and Matthew. "I'm sorry I am late. A child fell and gashed his head, so I stopped to help. Judas and Matthew—these people are terribly tired and hungry. They need food and water, but how in the world can we manage? We barely have enough for ourselves."

The men nod with discouragement, and the four trudge up to meet Jesus and the others. Jesus has stopped speaking and smiles in greeting to Joanna as she sits beside him. Judas approaches. "Jesus, everyone is tired and hungry. We need to dismiss these people so that they can go to the villages and buy food for themselves."

"There is no need for them to go away," says Jesus. "Give them our food."

Peter protests, "But five loaves and two fish are all we have here. They will barely feed us, much less everyone here."

"Now, Peter. Bring me the loaves and the fishes along with some empty baskets. We'll see what we can do."

"But Jesus!"

"Peter, do you trust me?"

"Yes, Lord, I trust you. But there are hundreds of people here," he grumbles to himself.

Peter, Judas, Matthew, and Joanna each gets a basket and puts a loaf of bread and a piece of fish into each one. Jesus raises his eyes to heaven in silence. He then stretches his hands over the baskets and prays, "Blessed are you, Infinite One, who bring forth bread from the earth. Father, hear my prayer for these poorest of thy people. Give them the bounty of your seas and skies." He lowers his arms. "Now, each of you take a basket and offer the people something to eat."

They fan out, carrying the baskets. As they each start down a different side of the hill, hands reach in and pick out chunks of bread and fish. As soon as those nearby realize that food is being handed out, they begin to jostle, shove, and grab until finally the disciples lose their grips on the baskets and end up following the baskets as they are handed person to person all the way down to the bottom. The disciples and Joanna are unable to keep up. When

Peter and the others finally reach the bottom of the hill, there are four baskets full of bread and fish waiting for them.

"I don't understand," says Judas. "How did we end up with so much food?" All four are puzzled and confused.

"Well," says Matthew, "maybe people got generous, and when they saw our gift of bread and fish, they decided to share also."

Peter shakes his head. "That can't be right. Even a crowd this size wouldn't have this much food. It must be Jesus' doing. He prayed over the food, blessed it, and it multiplied until all were fed."

Judas scoffs. "That would be as great a miracle as the manna in the desert."

"So what's your explanation, then?" asks Matthew.

Judas just shrugs.

Peter's face turns solemn and stern. "This was more than just sharing. Most of these people had nothing to give, yet all were filled. Isn't Jesus always saying to rely on the Lord? We are full of doubts, but Jesus has no doubts. He calls on the Lord and is answered." The others shift uneasily, staring at the baskets. "Now let's redistribute this food so that everyone can have some for their journey home."

Sometime later, Joanna sits next to Jesus eating her portion of bread and fish. Thoughts swirl through her head as she, too, tries to figure out what has just happened. Did everyone start sharing, or were the loaves really multiplied by divine intervention? And if it was divine intervention then who is Jesus really? At times, he seems so ordinary, but sometimes he is extraordinary. She turns to look at him. He is talking softly to Rina and offering her a piece of bread. It is completely natural and familiar. But where did all the bread and the fish come from? And why would this be the day that God would choose to intervene with a miracle?"

The next morning, Joanna and Rina wake up and join Peter's mother as she cooks barley over the fire. They greet one another as Joanna squats down to take over the stirring.

"It will be a fine day today. Not too hot, I think," says Miriam.

"Yes, I think so too," agrees Joanna. She looks around. "Where is everybody? Did we oversleep?"

Miriam laughs. "No, the men just got up early to take Jesus to the other side of the lake. They wanted to get up and go before anyone else could follow them." She nods, and Joanna turns and sees a small group of men already waiting clustered on the road. "Capernaum is overflowing with people from the countryside who have come to see Jesus. He needs time to pray and rest, yet these people give him no peace!"

Rina is anxious. "Jesus is coming back, isn't he?"

"Of course, child. He just needs some peace and quiet! Don't worry, he will return."

Joanna, Miriam, and Rina eat their breakfast. As they eat, the street continues to fill, and the people spill toward the lake. Everyone is talking about Jesus and the loaves and fishes. The women finally get up, driven inside by all the noise and the curious onlookers.

Midafternoon, Jesus and the disciples return to the small harbor and collect Joanna and Rina, and all walk through the marketplace on their way to the synagogue.

As they walk, Judas tries to get Jesus' attention, but he can't be heard because of the crowd following them. He grabs Jesus' arm and leans in close. "Jesus, I must speak to you," he says.

"Certainly, but later, when the crowd is not so close by."

Judas nods and turns away.

Joanna is walking several yards ahead of Jesus on the edge of the crowd, holding Rina close. Suddenly, she sees a woman's huddled form lying on the ground. The crowd is almost trampling her, and Joanna and Rina lean down over the woman to shield her. Just as Jesus passes by, the woman reaches out and grabs the hem of Jesus' garment. Immediately, Jesus turns around, looking intently at the crowd milling about.

"Who touched my garment?"

Peter answers, for he has never heard Jesus sound so stern. "Master, you see the crowd pressing in on you, and you say, 'Who touched me?' It could have been anyone."

"Peter," explains Jesus, "I felt the power go out of me." He turns and says again, louder this time, "Who touched my garment?"

The woman struggles to her feet with Joanna and Rina's help. She is bent over, trembling with fear. Jesus comes near and takes her hands. She tries to pull away, but Jesus holds her firmly. She swallows and admits, "Lord, I am the one who touched your garment. I have been sick for twelve years." She hangs her head in shame, unable to meet Jesus' eyes. She whispers, "Nothing can stop my bleeding, so I have to live apart. My family has spent everything they have on doctors, but no one can help me. I knew that if I could just touch your garment, I would be healed."

Jesus puts his hand under her chin and lifts her head so that their eyes meet. The woman's fears seems to ebb away as she sees the compassion and intense love on Jesus' face. "Daughter," he says, "what is your name?"

"Sara'el, Lord."

"Sara'el, your faith has made you well; go in peace and be healed of your affliction."

For a moment, the woman does not react, stunned as she is by Jesus' words. Then she feels the healing warmth that runs through her body. Suddenly, she shouts, "Jesus, Lord, I give you praise and thanks. You have driven out the illness. I am cured! I am cured!"

As she says these words, the woman stands straight without help, though obviously weak. Tears run down her face. The crowd begins to murmur as the news spreads of the healing. The people press closer and closer to Jesus, and Joanna and Rina continue to prop the woman up so she is not trampled. The disciples push the crowd back to create a little space.

Joanna looks at Jesus. "Lord, I would like to take her back to her home. She is still too weak to walk by herself, and I would like to speak to her family about how to best care for her after this long illness."

Jesus nods, smiles at the woman, and continues onward. The crowd flows after Jesus, leaving the three alone. Unsure of her footing, Sara'el slowly and falteringly leads Joanna and Rina down a small road, through a gate, and into a large courtyard. There are two houses to one side, with an outdoor kitchen between them. The animal pens are mostly empty, and the yard is surrounded by a low stone wall, crumbling and in disrepair. It is obvious that once the family was well off, but no more.

At Saraèl's cries of jubilation, family members stop their work and cluster around. There is love on their faces, but Joanna notices that they refrain from touching her. "Fear not," Saraèl cries. "My illness has been cured! I am no longer unclean! Jesus, my Lord, has done this. As I touched his garment, I felt a tremendous warmth and the strength of his power. My bleeding has stopped. Finally, after all this time, I am cured!"

The family group starts to pepper Saraèl with questions so fast that she cannot begin to answer them.

Joanna holds up a hand to interrupt. She grins at the happiness on their faces. "My name is Joanna, and this is Rina. We wanted to bring her home to make sure she reached home safely. She is still very weak. Please fetch the rabbi. She will need the prayers and ritual cleansing. First, perhaps we can bring her into the house to bathe her and get her something to eat." A young boy runs off to fetch the rabbi while everyone asks to hear the story again.

"In a minute, everyone. First I want to show Joanna where I have been living." Saraèl leads Joanna and Rina over to a tiny shed hidden behind the animal pens in the far corner. She shows them her mat of hay and her eating utensils. The smell is rank, and the scent of illness and old blood hangs in the air. Joanna is struck forcibly by the stench and the almost palpable spirit of despair and loneliness. Rina feels it, too, and starts to cry in sympathy for the desperate life that Saraèl has endured.

The woman pats Rina, saying, "Don't cry, little one. It's all over now. Blessed be God forever."

An hour later, the rabbi exits the main house followed by the men in the family, who see him to the gate. The women follow but turn to one side. Joanna starts to give some instructions. "She will be weak for some time, and her strength needs to be built up slowly. She needs to eat plenty of eggs and chicken, mutton, and even goat in a week or two. Watered wine to start, of course."

As Joanna continues talking, Rina takes the medical bag from around her neck and selects a small brown vial. Joanna says, "Here is some medicine to help strengthen the blood. She should have one small dose in the morning and one at night."

Sara'el's oldest sister nods. "We will do our best for her, but as you can see, we have no animals. We just eat mostly grains now. Our sheep are long gone, and we have no money to buy any. They are too expensive for us now, much less good wine or goat!"

Joanna and Rina exchange a look and have no need for words. Rina reaches into the bag again and selects a small knife, which she hands to Joanna. Joanna takes it, turns her back from where the men are standing, and cuts out some of the pouches sewn into her skirt. Joanna continues her instructions. "Take this money and buy some of what you need. Put it to good use, and it should be enough to see you through the next few months. I'm sure your fortunes will recover, since you no longer need to pay doctors. We join you in giving thanks for God's providence."

Sara'el and her sisters embrace Joanna and Rina as they leave through the crumbling gate.

Still unused to speaking, Rina is a silent partner on the walk back, and Joanna's thoughts are full of the miraculous events of the last few days. As they walk back into town, she struggles to understand Jesus' power and purpose. Jesus preaches about repentance, but his healings do not require an admission of sin. Aren't people ill because they have sinned? And the multiplication of the loaves and the fishes was purely a gift to everyone there. No one earned it or had to work to deserve it. The disciples speak of Jesus as the Son of God. But how could that be? Generations have waited for a savior. Why would the savior be here? Why now? Her thoughts swirl back and forth as they walk.

X

As they near Capernaum, Joanna sees a group of men in the road. Remnants of a crowd trail off into the distance, but a small group remains. The men are quite excited, gesticulating and arguing loudly. Joanna gestures to Rina to stop, not wanting to get too close. Joanna recognizes the rabbi who performed the cleansing ritual for Sara'el and then she sees Jairus, her ex-brother-in-law, who is standing at the center of the group. When Joanna recognizes him, she turns away quickly and walks back the other way to keep from being recognized, but Jairus sees her and calls, "Joanna! Joanna!"

When she hears her name, she grabs Rina's hand and walks even faster, but Jairus soon catches up with her.

He is bursting with excitement. "Joanna, I thought it was you. What are you doing here?" He doesn't stop to hear her answer. "But never mind, I must tell you! Have you heard? Have you heard? Have you heard about my daughter?"

"What about Ariyah? Is she alright? What has happened?"

"She has been so ill, Joanna. A fever clung to her so hard she could barely breathe. We were frantic, and the physicians could do nothing. We have spent three days watching her life ebb away. She could not eat. She could not drink. Today, I couldn't bear it any longer. I ran out of the house, desperate for help. I saw the crowd with Jesus, so I ran up to him, shouting. I begged him to help us. He came at once with a disciple. We were arriving at the house when my steward found us and said that Ariyah had died."

Joanna gasps and clutches Rina to her side.

"My anguish was so great I could barely stand, but Jesus said, 'Your child is not dead but asleep.' We pushed through the crowd. The weeping and wailing was so loud I will never forget it. My little girl was dead."

"Oh Jairus, how horrible," says Joanna. "I am so sorry."

"Ariyah was lying on her bed covered with a thin blanket. There was no breath, no life. Phoebe was clinging to her body, sobbing. Then Jesus went to the side of the bed and placed his hand on Phoebe's shoulder. 'Do not be afraid,' said Jesus. "You must have faith. Your daughter is not dead; she is only sleeping."

"What happened next?" asks Rina. "What did Jesus do? Did he help her?"

Jairus continues his story. "The wailing gradually died away as the disciple convinced the mourners to leave. Finally, there was this deep silence; even Phoebe had stopped crying. Then Jesus knelt down and laid his hands on Ariyah's head. I could hear Jesus breathe in and out, in and out, slowly, very slowly. Then he leaned over her until his lips touched her mouth; there was only the sound of that breath—breath in and out, in and out. Then he drew back and said, 'Talitha koam.' I heard a small, tiny gasp and a breath join his. It was Ariyah's. Her chest began to rise and fall, and color returned to her face. I couldn't believe it. One moment she was dead, the next moment she was alive. Phoebe and I were frozen in astonishment. When she opened her eyes, Jesus said, 'Welcome, daughter. You have been very ill. You are probably hungry. Someone, please get her some water and a little bread soaked in milk.' While we clung to Ariyah, full of gratitude for her recovery, Jesus and his disciple slipped out. We never even got a chance to thank him."

"Jairus, I rejoice with you, Rebecca, and your whole family. God's power is great, and he works through Jesus."

"Yes, I know that now. I was so blind before. I am embarrassed by the way I treated him at my house. I must tell everyone." Jairus continues, gesticulating excitedly, "Jesus is a great prophet. It was a miracle, a true miracle. I just didn't understand. The hand of God is truly upon him."

"I have seen his healing powers myself. He cured my little girl. She was dumb, and now she can speak." Joanna pulls Rina in close.

Suddenly, Jairus realizes that Joanna is far from home and, chagrined, remembers that Chuza has divorced her. Joanna watches as his face turns red from embarrassment. "Oh, Joanna, I just remembered—the divorce. And isn't this your servant? We have been wondering what became of you. You must be traveling through Galilee to go to family. Are they nearby?"

"No, Jairus. I was originally from Jaffa, but I have no family left there. Rina and I are on our own. And Chuza has chosen another. It was a terrible shock to me, but I am beginning to make a new life for myself. I'm not here to impose on your family. Right now, we are traveling with Jesus and his disciples, helping him at the request of a friend of mine."

Jairus is astonished. "But how can that be? You are unaccompanied?"

Joanna nods.

"You are not accompanied by any relative at all! And the crowds! This is awful. Even though you are barren, Chuza was sure that someone else would have married you," he said with pity in his voice. "We did talk about it—perhaps a widower who needed a mother for his children—but no one will marry you now. Your life—it is ruined."

"Jairus, peace. I am not your responsibility. Chuza threw me away. So be it. Now I live the way I choose to live. I make my own living, and I am raising Rina the best way I know how. And right now, we are following Jesus back to Magdala. Besides, don't forget what Jesus has done for you. Be grateful and give thanks to God. You have been given a most blessed gift."

"Certainly, we will make a thanksgiving offering to the synagogue, but I also want to contribute to Jesus' teaching and ministry. Could you deliver this for me?" Jairus hands Joanna a bag of coins. "Please accept these coins for Jesus in gratitude for all that he has done for us." Then he hands her another small bag. "And here is some money for you—for clothes, or food, or whatever else you need. I would invite you to stay, but . . ."

"It's alright, Jairus. I know your wife and mother wouldn't welcome us. Divorce doesn't just separate two people; it separates entire families. I will pray that Ariyah and your entire family will continue to be well." She and Rina leave, Jairus looking after them as they continue down the road.

That night after the evening meal, everyone is relaxing and enjoying the slight breeze blowing up from the water. Judas beckons to Joanna to follow him, and they both approach Jesus.

"Master, may I speak with you?"

Jesus nods.

"I have observed something which needs your attention. I have seen that Joanna is keeping money for herself instead of sharing it with all."

Joanna stiffens with anger and resentment. She starts to speak, but Jesus makes a small gesture to stop her.

"You know that she gave you the money from Jairus. I saw her give it to you myself," Jesus replies.

"Not that money. She has money sewn into her skirt. I don't know where she's gotten it. For all I know, she kept some of Jairus' money for herself. This is not fair. We share, and share alike. It creates resentment and discord when some of us have means and some have not."

Jesus lays a hand on Judas's shoulder. "I don't think we need to worry. Her needs as a healer and midwife are unique, and she puts herself and her knowledge at our disposal. Herbs, ointments, and bandages are all expensive. It seems to me that we benefit a great deal from Joanna's presence with us."

"But that doesn't mean she can just keep the money that rightly belongs to all of us!" Judas says.

"Judas," Jesus says, "Joanna is here as a favor to us. She does not need to follow our ways of doing things. Don't forget that she is not a disciple and that she has a child. And as far as resentment goes, no one else needs to know, if you choose to not tell anyone."

He gives Judas a stern look. Judas bows in acquiescence, but his shoulders remain hunched as he stalks away.

Jesus and Joanna look at one another. Joanna starts to say something, but Rina comes up and interrupts them. Both Jesus and Joanna say goodnight to her and then move a little closer to the fire.

Joanna speaks softly to keep from being overheard by those who are still awake. "Thank you for what you said. I really didn't take the money from Jairus. I gave it all to Judas. I even gave him the money that Jairus gave me because his brother cast me out."

Jesus is silent.

"But he is right—I do have money, but it is the money I made when I sold my clothes and my jewelry in Tiberius. Some of the money is sewn into my skirts, and some is still buried in Magdala."

Jesus still doesn't respond.

Joanna shifts uneasily, aware that she is becoming nervous but not knowing why. To fill the silence, she speaks rapidly, almost babbling. "I met Jairus in the street as we were returning. He was trying to convince the elders of his daughter's healing. He is so grateful to you; their whole family is."

Jesus looks away and pokes at the coals with a long stick. The firelight flickers over his face.

Still nervous, Joanna blurts out, "I know that you and the disciples will be leaving tomorrow for Caeserea, and after that you will be returning for Magdala on your way to Jerusalem."

"Yes," says Jesus, "Jerusalem for the Passover. The crowds filling the city are always large." His voice trails off.

Joanna notices the sadness on his face, which is barely lit by the dying coals. Joanna plucks at her cloak uneasily. She swallows a couple of times.

"Well, I think you should know that I have decided to return to Magdala. I'm thinking of Rina. I hope to establish myself as a midwife there so that I can raise her properly. Mary said she would help me. I was pleased to be able to help you with Susanna, and traveling along, I have learned a lot, but I think a quiet and steady, homebound life would be best."

"That sounds like a sensible plan."

"Yes, a home of one's own is very important, especially for a child."

"Yes, a home of one's own to lay down one's head," he agrees. "I think often of my home in Nazareth."

They are both silent again. Finally, Joanna blurts out, "When I was a child, I felt close to God. My mother and father were very observant—the feast days, the prayers, the rhythms of belief. And after my parents died and I was married, I felt that my life as a wife and my work as a midwife bound me closer to God. Even though many in the palace, including my husband, did not really believe, I could feel and see the grace of God in those around me." Joanna pauses to find the words for what she wants to describe. "But ever since my divorce, that connection to grace is gone. God is very distant. I say the prayers, I perform the good works, but there is only a silence. I am ashamed much of the time, and I have become hardened. Sometimes I feel as if my entire heart has shriveled. I am no longer myself."

Jesus looks up from the flames and into Joanna's eyes. His voice is gentle. "This is when faith and belief in God is the hardest. When we can't seem to hear his voice; when we can't feel his presence." Jesus quotes, "'He blinded their eyes and hardened their heart, so that they might not see with their eyes or understand with their heart.' That's what the prophets say."

Joanna grimaces and then smiles ruefully. "But I don't want this silent separation. I want to be as before. I am surrounded here by such strong faith—James, John, and Peter, and of course Mary. But there is a veil that separates me from them. I don't know what it is."

"Obedience to God's will, especially if it is in silence, is asked of all us. And don't forget the end of the passage. 'They might not see with their eyes or understand with their heart, but I will heal them, says the LORD.' Don't forget, Joanna, your training as a midwife. Some healing takes time; some happens in an instant."

Joanna's eyes fill with tears and she feels bereft, but she doesn't know exactly why.

X

Jesus continues, "I will pick a disciple to go back with you. You shouldn't travel the road alone."

"Oh no, Jesus. I can't let you do that. The men need to go with you. We shall be fine. It will only take a couple of days, and we will find a family to walk with if need be."

"Very well, if you are sure."

"I'm sure. We will definitely be alright."

There seems to be nothing more to say, and they both turn their attention to the embers, which are collapsing into ash.

The next morning, the women are preparing breakfast. Joanna listens absentmindedly to Miriam's chatter. The disciples, too, are bustling and talkative, eager to be off. She notices that only Jesus is distracted and ill at ease. He leaves the group and walks down to the shore, staring at the water.

Peter starts organizing. "We'll travel for two months around Caesarea Philippi and then return to Magda. At Mary's, we will rest a little and pack the supplies for our travel to Jerusalem. Oh, on second thought, all we will need to do is lie about, because Mary will already have everything organized and packed up, since she plans on coming with us. The only thing that will be left for us to do is fill the waterskins."

The other disciples laugh and nod.

Thaddeus stands, throwing his arms out wide. "Then, on to Jerusalem! Of course, the news of Jesus will travel before us. It will be even more chaotic than last year—dustier, louder, and encounters with . . ." He points to various disciples one by one as they chime in.

"Believers."

"Skeptics."

"Revolutionaries."

"Naysayers."

And then they all shout together, "Pharisees!"

Sobering, Thaddeus continues, "And we can't forget the Romans and all those who wish to be healed. There will be a lot of work for each one of us."

Joanna listens as Judas continues. "There will certainly be active opposition from the Sanhedrin. They will never accept Jesus as the Son of Man, no matter how much support we have from the people. They will label us as blasphemers and false witnesses, just as they did before. But when Jesus reveals his real power, this time it will be different. Then all arguments will be over!"

Peter shakes his head in disagreement. "Jesus will never perform miracles on demand or on his own behalf. He has no use for that kind of power. He wants to change hearts, not rule people. He wants repentance and a return to the Father, not crowns and diadems."

John adds, "But there is no telling what the Romans will do if there is unrest. They are so nervous at Passover. They might take their uneasiness out on anyone who is drawing crowds; and Jesus is sure to draw crowds."

The mood sobers as breakfast is passed around. John leads the blessing, and they all begin to eat. Jesus rejoins the group, accepts a plate, and takes a bite of fish. "Hmm, good. Thank you." He continues to talk while he eats. "My mother will be traveling with some neighbors up to Jerusalem and should arrive around the same time as we will, I hope. It has been so long since we have seen her, and we have need of her gentle grace, don't you think?"

All smile and nod enthusiastically, except for Joanna, who pulls Peter aside. "Peter, Jesus has a mother? I didn't know that."

Peter smiles at Joanna's amazement. "Of course he has a mother. Her name is Mary, and she lives in Nazareth. Her husband Joseph died ten years ago. She is an amazing woman and very close to God. We all love her very much. Jesus has other family too. You have heard of John the Baptist?"

Joanna nods.

"He was Jesus' cousin."

"Wasn't he the wild prophet in the desert? We got the news in Tiberius that Herod had him beheaded. I've always been afraid of Herod. He has an atrocious temper, and he is often paranoid. I always tried to stay as far away from him as possible.

Peter's eyes fill with tears. "John was a fearless preacher. Many went out into the desert to seek him out. They confessed their sins, and he baptized them. He even baptized Jesus; he was tireless. He had one focus—to convince the whole world to repent in preparation for the Messiah. Some of us were his disciples at first, but he told us to follow Jesus instead." Peter pauses, sorrow lining his face. "His death still shakes us, and no one grieves more than Jesus. John preached too many times about Herod's illicit marriage. Even in prison he continued. And he continues to teach us by his life and by his death. We all know the risk is real."

Joanna is anxious and confused as she tries to make sense of all that Peter has said. Her heart goes out to Jesus and the other men. She feels an irrational desire to stay with the group, to help with their sorrows and their challenges, but believes that she owes Rina another kind of life.

As they return to the group, Jesus is speaking. "Joanna has decided that it is time to return to Magdala. She has been a great deal of help to all of us, and we thank her."

The disciples clap softly and grin.

"And Rina, you have been such wonderful company. We shall miss you greatly and hope to see you again in Magdala."

Rina blushes, smiles, and then looks at Jesus wistfully, but she says nothing.

X I

An hour later, all are gathered in the street next to Peter's mother's house. Some have bundles; some have walking sticks. Joanna has their belongings slung over her back along with two days' worth of food for the journey, and as usual, Rina has a firm grip on the medical bag.

Joanna approaches Jesus. "Jesus, may we please have your blessing before we go?"

All of the disciples gather round. Jesus places one hand on Joanna's shoulder and extends his other hand over the men. His voice rolls over them. "May it be your will, my Father, that you should lead us in peace, guide us in peace, and support us in peace. Save all your servants from every enemy and ambush and from all kinds of punishments and rage that comes into the world. May you confer blessing upon all those here and grant them grace, kindness, and mercy. Blessed are you, Father, who hearkens to prayer." He lowers his hands and then squats down in front of Rina. He gently picks up one of her hands and then the other. "And this, dear Rina, is a blessing just for you." He closes his eyes, and Rina does too. "Bless this little lamb, who is so dear to all of us, and keep her safe in her mother's care. Amen."

Everyone echoes, "Amen."

There is a flurry as all take leave of one another. There are small bows and waves all around. John hugs Joanna, and James ruffles Rina's hair. The men turn north, and Joanna and Rina watch them go. Joanna's eyes fill with tears as she watches the familiar figures leave. But her eyes linger longest on Jesus, his back straight and stride purposeful.

"Mother, why are you crying? We will see Jesus again soon."

"Oh, I don't know, really. It is just sad. I was thinking about all that has happened since we left Magdala."

"But why would that make you cry?"

"I think I am crying because of the beauty of everything." She hugs Rina as hard as she can, and Rina gives a little "ooff." Joanna laughs, and they turn south, but the tears still fall.

Joanna and Rina arrive at Mary's gate in Magdala two days later. They are tired and look forward to seeing Mary and giving her their news before they go on to their little house by the water. Mary is at the well in the courtyard, and as she turns around, she sees them. She sets aside the water and hurries to meet them, hugging them as she speaks.

"Hello, hello. You are back! How was the trip? Has Susanna had her baby yet? Are the men with you, or did you come by yourselves?"

Joanna laughs and returns the hug. She has forgotten how vibrant and forceful Mary is. "Yes, we are back. Susanna is safely in her new home, but labor hasn't started yet. At least, I think it hasn't. And no, the men are not here. They are going to spend a couple of months around Caesarea Philippi before returning here, but their plan is still to go on to Jerusalem for Passover."

Mary draws them over to the well, urges them to sit, and offers them water to drink.

"Thank you," says Rina.

Mary is astonished and almost drops the cup. She stares at Rina in wonder. Rina giggles at the look on her face.

"Anat, you are talking. I can't believe it! How did this happen?"

All three look at each other and say at the same time, "Jesus!"

Rina explains in her soft, accented voice. "He told me a story about a lost lamb, and then he put his fingers on my mouth, and all of a sudden I could talk again."

Joanna puts her arm around Rina and explains about Rina's life before coming to the palace. "And now we know that Anat's real name is Rina. We have decided to adopt one another. We are mother and daughter now, not mistress and servant."

"Yes, I see that. We must celebrate. It's almost midday. Please stay for a meal before you return home."

"I'll get the food," offers Rina.

"Wonderful," says Mary. "There is some bread, dried fish, and I think there are figs . . . Oh, whatever you can find."

Rina nods happily, puts the medical bag on the ground, and goes inside. Both women watch her with smiles on their faces. Joanna stretches and then relaxes back against the tree nearest the well, relieved to have arrived safely.

"Rina is much happier now that we are a family, and I am too. But I worry about taking care of her. We don't have much of a home, or security for that matter."

"But Joanna, you and Rina can stay with me as long as you like. Magdala can be your new home permanently. You will even be doing me a favor, since you can watch the house while I am gone."

"That is very generous of you, but our shed on the beach will do for now. I know that you told me that there is a midwife here, but I have also heard that she is old and becoming unable to manage the long hours and strenuous work."

"Well, that is true. Razili is less and less able to manage, but she is very proud and would not take kindly to being supplanted by a young stranger. She is much appreciated by the people, and they would not take it kindly either if you suddenly set up shop."

"So, some diplomacy and tact is called for," said Joanna.

Mary makes a wry face. "A lot of diplomacy and a lot of tact. But tell me about your trip. How is Susanna? How did you get along with Jesus and his disciples?"

"Susanna is fine. The two women who offered her a home are very kind, and they should all do well together. They like the children and welcome their energy. She still hadn't gone into labor when we left, but the two women felt confident that between the two of them they could handle the birthing. As for Jesus and his disciples, it was a confusing, challenging, but wonderful time." Her voice trails off.

Just then, Rina arrives carrying a tray of food.

"Confusing and challenging? That sounds about right, but now let's eat. We can talk more later."

While they eat, Rina tells Mary about the little boy who hit his head on the rock, not realizing that perhaps stories about copious amounts of blood do not go well with bread and fish. Both women appreciate her matter-of-factness, but Joanna notes that she will need to explain about polite conversation to Rina. Then, almost in mid-sentence, Rina falls asleep, worn out from all the walking and the heat of the day. Joanna gets up and places her cloak under her head and makes sure she is in the shade. Mary collects the tray, and both women go into the house, coming back out a moment later carrying cups of watered wine. They settle down for a long talk.

"You wanted to know about Jesus and the disciples. They are well—much as they were when we left. I know that the brothers were glad to be able to drop Nahash off at home. She complained, but I know that secretly, she was glad to be in familiar surroundings. The traveling was hard on her.

"As for the men—I don't think that Judas likes me much, but the others were very considerate, and they were so kind to Rina. The trip was a lot of hard work and most especially on Jesus, of course. His preaching is drawing even bigger crowds, and at one point he had to actually get into a boat to preach because the crowd had almost pushed him into the water. There were remarkable cures. Rina, of course, and one was of my niece, who had a deadly fever."

"Were you there? Did you see it?"

"No, but I heard the story from my former brother-in-law. He was convinced that his daughter was dead before Jesus said she was just sleeping."

"That must have been hard, speaking to a member of your former family."

"Yes, for a while he was so excited and happy that he forgot that Chuza and I were no longer married. I told him that I was accompanying Jesus temporarily, and he was horrified, but no matter."

"And what did you discover about Jesus?"

Joanna struggles to describe her observations of Jesus. "Sometimes, Jesus sinks into such silence it's as if he is not aware of any of us, but at other times he is so sensitive he can feel the slightest touch. Sometimes he is the merriest of us all, but then he takes himself off as if he can't bear even one more conversation or joke. But I suppose it is natural, because the leadership and responsibility is all his, as you know. His connection to God is difficult for me to comprehend, but it is rich and deep."

"Was there any ill feeling from the local leaders?"

"Some who have witnessed the miracles believe, and some who have witnessed the miracles don't. Some resist his prophetic voice. They are not used to the intimate way he preaches about God. It makes them uneasy, and they accuse him of blasphemy. But others are inspired and feel a sense of hope and even a sense of freedom."

"And what about you? What do you think?"

Joanna smiles and pauses to think. "I am trying to figure that out. I trust in Jesus; I really do. But it is complicated. I can't seem to reconcile the contradictions—how can he be the one the Jews have been waiting for all this time?"

There is a long silence, and Mary waits patiently and does not interrupt.

"Jesus is human, but sometimes there is a look in his eyes that shows that he is seeing far beyond the rest of us. He talks with God, and he talks about God the Father as if he knows him. Love just pours out of him. But he does so many things that contradict custom and religious law. He eats and drinks with outcasts. He is not prudent. He challenges the Pharisees at every turn. He is such a mix of contradictions. He can cure all kinds of infirmities but has no interest in politics or government. Shouldn't he be working against Roman occupation? He can motivate huge crowds of people even to the point of revolt. Isn't that the way a savior of his people would act? Shouldn't he be urging the people to rise up?"

"Yes," says Mary. "We all have ideas about the way a true savior would act."

Joanna goes on. "I was so sure that it was the right thing to do to return here and set up a permanent home. Practical, responsible—but when we left Jesus, it was if my heart was split in two. All I could do was cry. I think I scared Rina. I couldn't stop crying."

Before Mary can respond, Rina wakes up. After promising to come back the next day, Joanna and Rina thank Mary for her hospitality, leave the courtyard, and continue on their way.

A week later finds Joanna and Rina stopping in front of a small, well-tended house adjacent to the road. An elderly man sits on a bench by the front door. He is small, gnarled, and severely bent over. He leans on a small staff as he speaks to the small flock of chickens at his feet.

"Good morning, sir. Is this the house of Razili, the midwife?" asks Joanna.

"Humph," says the elderly man. "It's my house. And I'm busy."

Joanna and Rina give each other a look, and Joanna adopts a deferential air. "And it is a fine house, with such fine chickens!"

The man straightens a little. "You noticed my chickens, did you? My wife has no use for them, but they are my constant companions. All she wants to do is eat them!"

"Your wife—is she here?"

"Well, how should I know?"

Just then, a woman steps from the front door out into the courtyard, drawn by the voices. She gives the man an exasperated look. She, too, is small, but wiry. One eye is opaque with cataracts, but she has an air of confidence. "Yes, I'm here. I'm the midwife." She looks at Joanna with an experienced eye. "Well, you're not pregnant, so how can I help you?"

"Help?" the man yelps. "Most people can't be helped. They complain, moaning and groaning about everything. If it isn't one thing, it is another."

"Quiet, man," Razili interrupts. "We're trying to talk." She nods at Joanna and Rina. "Why don't you come inside? It will be easier inside. Not so many interruptions."

"Right," grumbles the old man. "Go ahead, go inside. I like chickens better."

Joanna and Rina slip by him and enter the main room. They sit at a large wooden table, which takes up most of the space. The room is pleasantly dim after the brightness outside.

"Well, what is it? I have a lot to do today."

Joanna starts the explanation that she and Mary worked out in advance. "I am wondering if you would consider taking me on as an assistant. I know something of midwifery, but I would like the chance to work with someone who can help me improve my skills."

"Why would I do that? I don't even know you. You aren't from here. Where are you from?"

"My daughter and I are from Tiberius. My name is Joanna, and this is Rina. We have moved to Magdala and are friends with Mary, the fishmonger. She can vouch for my character."

Razili purses her lips. "Well, that is something. But what makes you think I would need an assistant?"

Joanna considers her words carefully. This will be the tricky part. "I guess it's more that I need a teacher. And you know, you have a wonderful reputation. Mary has introduced me to many women who sing your praises. You would be helping me a great deal. It would be a true tzedakah, because I have no husband or brothers." She puts her arm around Rina. "We must make our own way in the world."

Razili thinks this over. "What do you have in mind?"

"Perhaps something like this could work. Naturally, first the women would come to you."

"Naturally."

"Over the course of the pregnancy, how many times do you usually visit to check on them?"

"About three."

"Right. Well, then maybe I could make some of those visits for you and report back. Then when the woman goes into labor, I could accompany you. I could learn how you prepare the woman and her relatives for the birth, what supplies are needed." As she talks, Joanna makes sure that the woman is accepting her ideas. "Then I would stay with the woman through the hours of labor and you could return home. I would send Rina to you when the birth is near, and then I would assist you as directed."

Razili gives Joanna and Rina a long glance. "I will need to think about this. I can't trust the women of this area to just anyone. But I am curious—what do you have in the leather bag, and why does your girl wear it around her neck?"

"Rina can show you. It is her special responsibility."

Rina takes the bag from around her neck and lays it on the table. She unties the leather thongs and checks the contents.

Before taking anything out, Rina says, "Do you have a clean cloth we can use? We used our last one for bandages."

"Are you saying that my table isn't clean? That it is dirty?" Razili stiffens with indignation.

Rina is confused and knows that she has made Razili angry but doesn't know why. She looks at Joanna for help.

"No, no, not at all," Joanna assures her. "It is just that I have trained her very carefully. And she tries to do everything just as I have taught her."

Razili sits back on her stool and glares at Rina. "And do you know why you should lay a cloth down first?"

Rina closes her eyes and quotes, "Lay the cloth down first to protect the bottles, herbs, and knives from any dirt or dust. Everything must be as clean as possible to insure the health of the mother and baby."

Grudgingly impressed, Razili says, "Yes, well, quite right." And she fetches a clean towel, which Rina arranges on the table.

Rina identifies each item as she takes it out. "Olive-oil ointment . . . tincture of hyssop . . . salt for cleaning the baby . . . oil lamp for light and flame . . . scissors . . . needle and thread . . . and, of course, the bandages and cloths are missing because we need to buy more." Finally, she takes out the set of knives folded in a small leather packet. Rina opens it, and the knives gleam dully in the dim light.

Razili looks at the knives closely and then points to the smaller, sharpest one.

"Have you ever used this one?"

"Yes," says Joanna.

"How many times?"

"Five."

"Did the mothers and babies live?"

"Not all of them. Three mothers died from loss of blood. One baby was born dead, and one baby died of a fever several days later."

"So three babies and two mothers survived," states Razili.

"Yes, three babies and two mothers."

Razili motions to Rina to put the supplies away. "You have taught your daughter well, which means that you will probably be an equally good student for me. I think we might get along well together. So how do you propose we handle the fees?"

Joanna pauses a minute. "I think that if we are paid in money, you should receive two-thirds of the payment. After all, it is your reputation that brings the work."

"Agreed. But what if we are paid in food, like bread, grain, eggs, or chickens?"

"I think the food should be divided in half. Half for you and half for us."

"No, I should get two-thirds of the food too."

Joanna laughs, enjoying the haggling. "I don't think so—exactly half. I have a growing child to feed. Besides, I think you already have plenty of chickens."

Razili's severe air softens, and she smiles. "Unfortunately, my husband won't allow those chickens to meet their fate. He has even named them. They are his delight, the silly man. But I agree; the food will be divided equally."

The three of them stand and formally embrace one another.

"We are agreed," says Joanna. "You have a new assistant and an assistant's assistant."

Razili smiles.

XII

Joanna sits on the edge of Mary's small fountain eating a midday meal of dates, bread, and cheese. Mary has taken Rina back to the marketplace with her, and Joanna is enjoying this moment of quiet to herself. As she eats, she thinks back over the past weeks since her partnership with the elderly midwife began. She smiles to herself. So far, she and Rina have been able to do their jobs of cleaning the marketplace and helping Razili at the same time, but she can foresee the time when the demands of birthing babies will make it impossible to keep their jobs at the market. Contentedly, she thinks of her small pile of coins buried in the tin box behind the shed. Pretty soon, they will be able to do midwifery full-time and then maybe buy a house—one with all its walls this time. Joanna gets up and takes the plate into the house, scrubs it, and leaves it to dry. She reaches for a cup and goes outside. The insects drone in the heavy heat. Most people in the village are inside, napping away the heat of the day. The commotion of the marketplace has faded away. Joanna bends and fills her cup. As she sits sipping her water, two mourning doves fly into the courtyard cooing. They peck at the ground, and Joanna admires their soft, gray feathers and their bright black eyes. The noonday light intensifies. The sun is so bright that she closes her eyes but is still able to see the brightness through her eyelids. Orange and yellow, the light begins to glow and pulse. A breeze brushes her cheek.

Gradually, she hears the sound of water dashing over rocks. When the breeze intensifies into a wind, the sound of the water gets louder and louder. Suddenly, she is engulfed in sound and the eddies of air. She drops the cup. Startled, her eyes snap open, expecting to see a storm, but the garden is as still and quiet as before. The doves are still pecking and searching for food. Wondering, Joanna drops her hand into the water of the fountain. It murmurs back at her. It seems as before, nothing unusual. Slowly, she lowers her head into the water. It is refreshing and cool. Her hair fans out, swirling around her face. She feels as if she is floating. When she needs to take a breath, she sits up and tilts her face to the sun. Water drips over her shoulders and down into her lap. Her mind is a soft blank, and she feels hollowed out.

Mary bustles into the courtyard, saying, "I left Rina at the neighbors'. She is playing with their girls. I hope that's alright." She takes a closer look at Joanna, who has not responded. Coming over, she sees that Joanna's clothes are soaked with water.

Joanna gazes off into the distance, seemingly unaware that Mary is speaking to her. She is silently crying. Mary kneels down and starts brushing the tears away. "What has happened, Joanna?" Mary whispers.

Joanna mutely shakes her head.

Mary sits quietly, holding her hand.

"I don't know," Joanna says. "There was a bright light, then wind and rushing water. It was like being visited by a storm. But when I opened my eyes, there was nothing there!" She shakes her head in bewilderment. "I don't understand. What was it? What does it mean?"

There are several moments of silence before Mary speaks. She chooses every word carefully. "I think time will tell. You don't have to figure it out right now. You need time to come back to yourself." She stands up and urges Joanna to stand also. "Come into the house and lie down for a bit."

Joanna slumps against Mary as if there is no energy left in her body. The tears continue to flow.

It is sunset several days later. Mary and Joanna linger on the lake's edge in front of Joanna's shed, enjoying the change of colors in the sky. They don't talk much. Joanna is still disoriented by her experience in the garden. She picks up a rock and throws it into the water. Mary's eyes trace the hills on the other side of the lake, imagining the small farms tucked away. Turning aside, they find a grassy spot above the waterline and sit down.

After a comfortable silence, Joanna turns to Mary. "You have never told me how you met Jesus."

"No. Some of it is hard to talk about. Words and explanations don't come easily."

Joanna seems surprised, because Mary usually has no trouble speaking her mind. But she respects Mary too much to pry. "You don't have to tell me."

"I would like to tell you, but it is a long story." She picks up a rock and rolls it between her fingers. "I was married to a good, good man—ten years. We grew up as neighbors, then we grew up as man and wife." She smiles as her eyes mist. "He made me laugh; he worked hard. We were prosperous and built our big house. We looked forward to children and a family, but the children never came. Joshua never held it against me, though. He would cradle me and tell me not to cry—that God would bless us someday. Then he would always add that he was childish enough for anybody."

Joanna feels a quick stab of envy for such a loving marriage.

"One day, Joshua and his men were caught out in a winter squall. The boat lost its mast, and Joshua was dragged overboard in the rigging." She swallows. "They brought his body home and laid it in the courtyard. There was a big gash on his head, but the blood had all washed away. His face was so peaceful, like he was sleeping. I sat by his body for hours waiting for him to wake up, but he never did. It happened three years ago." Her voice trails off.

"Oh Mary, I am so, so sorry." Joanna clasps Mary's hand as she continues.

"Somewhere in the days of mourning, I got very sick. Light started hurting my eyes. It would pierce into my head. I started to stay home during the day to avoid the light, and finally, I covered my windows so that no light could get through. I was unable to supervise the steward, and he started stealing from me. Finally, one of my husband's friends scared him off, and he and his wife helped keep the business going. But instead of things getting better, they got worse.

"I started hearing voices. Each voice was different. One of the voices was an old man who shrieked and groaned. One voice would always growl. One voice was an infant, and it would cry and cry. The others were women who would hum and drone on and on in words I couldn't understand. The baby—that was the worst. Day after day, night after night, there was nothing I could do to make them stop. They wouldn't let me rest. I couldn't eat; I couldn't sleep. One night in desperation, I ran out of the gate and started down the lane. I think I was trying to outrun them. But I hadn't gotten far before I saw a light shining at the far end of the street. The brightness shattered inside my head. I huddled in pain next to a wall, but the group with the lantern came closer and closer. I yelled for them to go away, to douse the light, but then I must have fainted."

The hand that Joanna is holding has turned rigid and clammy. Joanna strokes the back of it until it relaxes.

"When I awoke, a man was speaking. He spoke for several minutes, but I couldn't understand what he was saying. Then one of my voices growled and shouted, 'We know you. Why are you here? Leave us alone!' The infant voice started crying and wailing. I guess I started to spit and scratch. Jesus (for it was Jesus, I found out later) put his hands on my head and said, 'Be quiet!' The voices dulled somewhat but still complained, hissed, and wheedled. I could not control my body, and I couldn't stop the voices. I even spat in his face. Then Jesus grasped my shoulders, leaned over me, and prayed directly into my ear, 'I command you—leave this woman. All of you leave, now!'

"I guess I fell unconscious. When I woke up, several neighbor women were tending me. It was late afternoon, and I felt as weak as a newborn lamb, but the light coming in the windows didn't hurt my eyes. My head ached, but the voices were gone, and they have never come back.

"The next day, Jesus and some of the disciples came back to see how I was. I was almost back to normal and able to take part in the conversation. I was still shaky but felt at peace for the first time in a long time. Jesus seemed like such a gentle soul to me, even if he could cast out demons. So that was how I met Jesus. We have become fast friends since, and the group stays here whenever they are traveling past. I feed them and try to spoil them a bit. They have so little."

Joanna looks intently at Mary Magdalene. "And now who do you say Jesus is?"

"I know in my heart of hearts. He commands demons, Joanna. He heals the sick. He gives life. He lives peace and love for everyone. He is the Son of God. He is the Son of the living God."

Joanna and Mary stand and look at the water, which is glistening orange and pink. Their arms are entwined, and their hearts are too full for speech.

Late in the afternoon of the next day, Harmon and Joanna are scrubbing down the stall tables with salt and a bit of water. Rina is sweeping on the far side of the square. Suddenly, she gives a loud shriek, and Joanna whirls around, terrified. Then she starts laughing. Peter is twirling Rina up and down, around and around. Travel worn, Jesus and the disciples are laughing too.

James shouts, "Here we are at last! Did you miss us?"

Peter puts Rina down and tousles her hair. "What, Harmon, there is no more fish? What are we going to do? We're starving."

Joanna is still laughing. "We might be able to prevail on Mary to feed you."

The whole group starts to walk down the street. Rina runs ahead to let Mary know they are coming. Joanna and Jesus fall into step with one another. Remembering her conversation with Mary the night before, Joanna feels shy and awkward.

Jesus says, "I think Rina has grown in the past several weeks. She is looking healthy and happy."

"Yes, she is quite well."

Jesus looks at her intently. "And you, how are you?"

"The work with the local midwife is going smoothly, and I am still able to fit in cleaning the marketplace."

"And . . . ?"

They are interrupted by Rina and Mary rushing toward them. Mary embraces the disciples one by one, chattering and laughing.

She darts up to Jesus and takes his hands. She kisses them and then bows her head over them. "Welcome, LORD. It is good that you are here."

"Yes, it is wonderful to be back. But I'm afraid it is going to mean a great deal of work for you. Some of us are very hungry."

Mary laughs and turns away, pulling Andrew and James ahead. Rina takes Jesus' hand, and they all sweep through the gate.

The stars come out as everyone finishes eating. Several disciples pick up the dishes and pots and disappear into the house. The rest slip out for an evening walk by the lake. Jesus goes and sits on the rim of the fountain. He dips one of his hands in and swirls it. Joanna watches him from across the courtyard. Jesus looks up and smiles at her, and in that instant, she hears the rush of water and wind again.

XIII

———

Several days later, the men are collecting supplies and packing bundles. Mary is supervising. All are lighthearted and anxious to be off. Mary keeps looking for Joanna to say goodbye but can't find her anywhere. Right as they are about to leave, Joanna walks through the front gate.

"Joanna, where have you been? We wanted to say goodbye."

Joanna looks slightly embarrassed. "I've been to see Razili. I wanted to tell her that Rina and I will be gone for a while because we will be traveling to Jerusalem for Passover."

Mary flies to her, bursting with excitement, and gives her a fierce hug. All the men turn to stare at the hubbub. "Are you sure? Are you really sure you want to go with us?"

"I'm positive," says Joanna, "and Rina agrees. We want to come with you if you will have us."

Rina grins from ear to ear, shifting the bag around her neck.

"But first, there is something we need to do. Rina, hand me one of our knives and bring out our coin box."

Rina pulls the small tin box and one of the knives out of the leather bag. They walk across the courtyard where Judas is conferring with Jesus. "I have something for you, Judas." She squats down beside him and slices the money pouches out of her skirt. They fall to the dirt. She picks them up one by one and gives them to Judas. "One . . . two . . . three. That's all of them."

"And here is our buried treasure too," says Rina with a twinkle in her eye. She hands him the small box.

Joanna and Rina walk regally away, smiling to themselves, and Joanna overhears Jesus saying, "God will provide. And even better, I believe that two more members have just been added to our traveling party."

Several hours later finds the group on the path winding up through the small valley of the southernmost hills. Behind them, whenever they turn around, the Sea of Galilee glistens. They can see almost its whole length, the boats with their white sails like little triangles bobbing up and down. There is a slight breeze, and the cyclamen sway, scattered through the tall grasses. The group stops to rest and to drink some water. Black swallows dart back and forth overhead.

"Rabbi, please," says Mary, "give us a teaching." Jesus looks at the beauty around them.

Then he says, "Look up at the birds. They sow not; neither do they reap or gather into barns, and our heavenly Father feeds them. Are you not of much more value than they? Which of you by being anxious can add one cubit to the measure of his life?"

Some of the disciples nod thoughtfully in agreement.

Jesus stands up and walks a few steps away and crouches over a small patch of flowers. He swivels and looks at his followers. "Consider the lilies of the field, how they grow; they toil not, neither do they spin: yet I say to you, that even Solomon in all his glory was not arrayed like one of these." Then he stands, his face alight. "Do not be anxious, therefore, saying, 'What shall we eat?' or 'What shall we drink?' or 'How shall we be clothed?'" Your heavenly Father knows that you have need of all these things. But seek first his kingdom, and his righteousness; and all these things will be added to you."

Jesus turns and quickly strides off. The group scrambles to pick up their things, and they all hurry after him.

Joanna finds herself walking with Peter. "I have to admit I have a lot of anxiety—about the future, about Rina. After all, she is not a flower."

Peter nods. "It is natural to worry and plan. But I think Jesus is saying that we need to turn to God more in trust. Just relying on ourselves gets in the way of God's plans for us. But it is a hard teaching."

"A hard teaching . . ." echoes Joanna.

Days later, Jesus' group is spread along a well-trodden road winding through a rocky plain. They keep a steady pace, stopping for Jesus and the others to minister at the villages along the way and to sleep. They mostly eat while walking, knowing that the Passover is drawing near and wanting to make good time. Joanna often uses their brief rest periods to teach Rina more about midwifery. They work on plant identification and proper preparations for each one. The group stops for an hour or two at each village so that Jesus can deliver his message of God's mercy and compassion.

Sometimes their group is joined for a time by those inspired by Jesus' words. This day, Jesus is at the rear of the group talking with a man and his wife and their neighbor who have joined them from the last village. It is the Sabbath, and there is a sizeable town in the distance. Dark clouds tower in the sky. There are other people on the road hurrying along, hoping to reach shelter before the rains.

Peter, who is at the front of the group, notices a small group of religious leaders walking towards them—three Pharisees. He walks back and lays his hand on Jesus' shoulder. He indicates the group approaching. He says, "Jesus, I think there is a welcoming committee coming our way. I'm sure they don't want us to be caught in the rain. They are probably coming to offer us Sabbath hospitality."

"Peter, don't be sarcastic and don't borrow trouble. Let us listen to what our brethren have to say."

Just then, there is a shout of pain from a nearby field. An ox has kicked his plough over, and it has landed on the man working the field. Startled by the man's screams, the ox lumbers aside, dragging the plough off with him. All turn to help. Several of the disciples run after the ox and lead him back. Joanna and Mary step over the furrows and stoop over the man to see his injury. As Mary gives him a drink of water, Joanna examines his leg. The man grimaces and thrashes. His leg is obviously broken, and it is clear from the expression on Joanna's face that the break is serious.

She turns and looks at Jesus. "Master, this man is grievously hurt. Help him, please! The bone has broken the skin, and it is far beyond my ability to help."

As she is speaking, the religious men from the town reach the disciples.

As Jesus starts to bend down over the man, one of them objects, reaching out a hand in protest. "Jesus—you are Jesus, aren't you?—surely you mean to do no work today, healing or otherwise. This man is a Greek and does not live according to our laws, but you, as a Jew, must respect the observances handed down by our fathers."

Another says, "There are six days of the week for working, but the Sabbath is for God."

Jesus responds, "There is good and evil, life and death. It honors God more to do good and give life than to allow misery and pain."

"But the Sabbath law guides us in the good—not your imaginings about what God wants. The reports are true, then. You have no regard for the laws and the precepts of our faith. You place yourself above the tradition. You recognize no law but yourself, and you think you know the will of God."

Jesus answers angrily, "You hypocrites! Each of you works on the Sabbath day! Don't you untie your ox or your donkey from its stall on the Sabbath and lead it out for water? I obey my Father's will. My Father is still working, and I also am working."

The Pharisees begin to remonstrate with loud voices and gesturing. The disciples begin to shout back. Some shoving starts. Jesus stands and quiets both groups.

As Jesus continues to speak, the local leaders are visibly shocked. "Very truly, I tell you, the Son can do nothing on his own, but only what he sees the Father doing; for whatever the Father does, the Son does likewise. The Father loves the Son and shows him all that he himself is doing."

The Pharisees and the Sadducees are incensed. They spit on the ground at Jesus' feet. "Blasphemer! How dare you speak thus?"

Jesus' anger ebbs away. His face saddens, and he speaks with a low voice. "How dare you? You disregard God's action in the world but cling to human tradition."

The eldest Pharisee spits out, "Enough! We will not listen to drivel and lies. Do not dare to enter our town or we will set the dogs on you! And make sure the berth is wide. Our dogs do not like blasphemers or strangers!"

As Jesus stoops down to lay hands on the injured man, Peter turns to Matthew. "Was I right or was I right? It looks like we will be sleeping outside tonight."

Greatly upset by the confrontation, the three neighbors who joined the group earlier in the day stand by, murmuring. After several minutes, they slip away, too embarrassed to say anything to Jesus. The disciples are so busy praying with Jesus over the injured man they don't realize they have left.

The next day at noon, they are sitting in groups of two or three near some craggy boulders eating a light meal. The mud from the late winter deluge has already dried on the road, but some of their clothes are still wet. Most have shed their outer garments in order to dry them out.

Mary and Joanna sit together. "Yesterday was a hard day. I've rarely seen men so full of fear and hatred as from that town," says Joanna.

Mary agrees. "At one point, I actually thought it might come to blows."

Just then, a young man comes up to them, gasping for breath. "I have finally caught up with you! My servant is the man that you cured yesterday. I have come all this way. I want to learn more. Which of these men is Jesus?"

Mary points to Jesus.

The young man flings himself at Jesus' feet, prostrates himself, and then raises his head expectantly. "Rabbi, I know that you are a great teacher and healer. Your wisdom is known by many. My servant can walk now, despite his injury. It is said that you are the Son of Man. Please, can you teach me about God and eternal life? What good must I do?"

Jesus seems bemused by his enthusiastic questions but answers readily. "If you wish to enter into eternal life, you must keep the commandments."

"Which ones?"

Jesus answers, "You must not kill; you shall not commit adultery; you shall not steal; you shall not bear false witness; honor your father and your mother; and you shall love your neighbor as yourself."

The young man nods. "Good, then. I have obeyed these commandments since I was a child. Is there anything I lack?"

Jesus looks at him with pity. "My son, if you wish to be perfect, go, sell what you have and give it to the poor, and you will have treasure in heaven. And then when you have done that, come and follow me."

The man's face falls. "But Jesus," protests the young man, "this teaching is too harsh. Even if I wanted to, I cannot give my inheritance away. I am not like your other followers. I have family. Servants. Tenants. Responsibilities."

Peter, who has been listening and is still testy from the confrontation of the previous day, responds, "So what you are saying is that you have too much money to give it away. You think none of us have family, money, responsibilities? We have chosen this way."

The man's face is covered in confusion and embarrassment. His enthusiasm has disappeared, and he looks at Jesus. Finally, he slowly stands, bowing, and says to Jesus, "I am sorry, but this teaching is too difficult for me." He stands and goes back the way he came.

As he leaves, Joanna notices that Jesus sags a little against the boulder. The disciples gather around him as if to give him support.

Jesus says, "Well, I think we have rested long enough. Our clothes are mostly dry. But I think it is now time to leave Galilee. At the next opportunity, we will cross the Jordan and go down to Jerusalem through Samaria. It will be quicker."

There is a rumble of dissent from several disciples. Thomas voices what they are all thinking: "But Jesus, the Samaritans will have nothing to do with Jews."

Jesus heaves a heavy sigh. "Is that so different than here? Sometimes Jews will have nothing to do with Jews."

XIV

Four days later, Mary, Joanna, and Rina approach the outskirts of Sychar, a Samaritan town on the plains before the pass of Shecam. They come upon a cluster of small houses where women are weaving on small looms. The Samaritan women look at the strangers suspiciously. They can tell immediately that they are Jews. One older woman stands and goes into her house to avoid speaking to them.

"Good afternoon," says Mary. "We have come from the north and are on our way to Jerusalem."

There are silent stares from the group. In the silence, Joanna can hear the bleating of goats nearby and the shrill cries of children at play. "May we use your grinding stones? We will be glad to share the flour."

One of the women stands to speak with them. "Where are the men in your party"?

"They are still at Jacob's well."

Joanna explains. "We came ahead to see if we could renew our supply of flour. The journey from Galilee is long, and we need to supplement our food whenever we can."

"The grinding stones are over there. Don't be long about it. It is getting late." She and the other women continue their weaving, ignoring Mary and Joanna.

As Mary and Joanna begin to grind their sack of grain, Rina looks wistfully in the direction of the noises coming from the children.

"Rina, go ahead and join them, but leave the bag behind. I'll keep an eye on it," says Joanna.

Rina takes the medical bag off and runs off behind the houses. After several minutes, the sounds of play change. The shouts are louder and nastier, and suddenly, there is a shriek. Joanna recognizes Rina's voice and jumps up.

"Go and see to her, Joanna," urges Mary. "I'll keep working here, since we are running out of time."

Followed by one of the Samaritan women, Joanna runs toward the noises.

Rina is surrounded by children of varying ages. They are yelling at her and dashing in to snatch at her clothes. Some of the braver ones poke her while they mock her. Rina is frightened, and tears are running down her face. One boy stoops down to pick up a rock.

"Stop this right now! Leave her be," shouts Joanna. She rushes to Rina and embraces her after quickly checking to make sure she is not hurt.

The Samaritan woman starts cuffing the children nearest to her. "What do you think you are doing? Five against one. Stop it this instant."

The ringleader of the group excitedly explains, "But Samaritans have nothing to do with Jews! Why is she here? We don't want her!"

Another child pipes up, "Jews hate us, and we hate Jews."

The Samaritan woman shakes her head in disgust. "But that doesn't mean that you get to gang up on a little girl."

The children clearly don't feel sorry for what they have done. The look on their faces is defiant. Joanna leads Rina away, and the rest of the children and the woman follow them. Mary gets up and comforts Rina, and the three of them silently work to finish the grinding. The Samaritans watch them in varying degrees of hostility, embarrassment, and wariness. Almost finished, Joanna turns around.

"We travel with Jesus of Nazareth. Have you heard of him?"

Several of the women shake their heads no.

"He is a famous rabbi, and he tells a story about a Samaritan. Would you like to hear it?"

The woman who helped rescue Rina nods yes.

Joanna raises her voice a little so that everyone can hear. "A man was going down from Jerusalem to Jericho when he was attacked by robbers. They took his clothes, his money, and his donkey. Then they beat him, leaving him half dead by the side of the road."

The children draw nearer.

"A priest happened to be going down the same road, and when he saw the man, he passed by on the other side. So, too, a Levite, when he came to the place and saw him, passed by on the other side. But a Samaritan came to where the man was; and when he saw him, he took pity on him. He poured oil and wine over the cuts and bruises and bandaged his wounds. Then he put the man on his own donkey, brought him to an inn, and took care of him. The next day, he took out two denarii and gave them to the innkeeper. 'Look after him,' he said, 'and when I return, I will reimburse you for any extra expense you may have.'" Joanna looks at the children who, despite their animosity, are listening intently. Joanna continues. She looks at the children who have gathered closer. "Which of these three do you think was a neighbor to the man who was hurt by the robbers?"

The leader of the group of children says, "The Samaritan man. He was the good neighbor. He was the one who took care of the stranger."

"We must all try and be like that man. We should take care of one another no matter where we live or what tribe we belong to."

Just then, the group is disrupted by a Samaritan woman running toward them. She is panting and disheveled. She stops abruptly and motions for everyone to come closer. "I have just come from Jacob's well, and I talked a long time with a Jewish man who asked me for a drink of water."

"Do you honestly expect us to believe that? A Jewish man would never speak to you! This must be one of your famous stories," snorted one of the women.

"No, no, it's true."

"He spoke to you!? He asked you for a drink?" The women start to whisper in alarm.

Mary tries to calm them. "That is Jesus, our Lord and master. The one we follow. We are on our way to Jerusalem for Passover."

The woman continues to explain. "We talked a long time. He knew all about my past, and we have never even met! The most amazing thing he told me is that the hour is coming when we will not worship here on the holy mountain."

"He told you that we must worship in Jerusalem, didn't he? That's just like every other Jew I've ever heard," the oldest Samaritan woman snaps.

"No, he didn't. He said the hour is coming and is now here when true worshipers will worship the Father in spirit and truth and that it doesn't matter where you are. You must worship in spirit, he said, because God is Spirit. I told him that I knew that the Messiah is coming—the Anointed One—and that when he comes he will tell us everything. Jesus said then, 'I am here.'"

There was derisive laughter from most of the women. One of the women snorted. "He said he was the Messiah? That's pretty hard to believe. I think you are just saying this to get attention. We are used to your lies."

"This is different. He knew all about my past—my husbands—even though I have never seen him before in my life! He knew I had five."

The women gather in closer, asking rapid-fire questions and trying to make sense of the story the woman has told. Mary and Joanna are peppered with questions also. They answer them as best they can. The witness interjects often with details and observations, elated with her experience. The grinding of the flour and the weaving of cloth are forgotten.

Just then, there is a lot of noise coming from the road. Jesus and his disciples are coming into town, and with them are some shepherds and their flocks. The shepherds are mocking the Jews and stirring up their flocks, making the disciples cough and sneeze in the ever-increasing dust.

The Samaritan woman runs up to Jesus and grabs his arms, pulling him toward the group of women. "See? This is him, the one I told you about—God's anointed."

Jesus laughs. "Wait, wait. Here is your jug. You left it by the well. We filled it for you." Jesus hands the sloshing jug over.

After locking their sheep in their pens, the shepherds join their wives, bristling at the sight of their women speaking with Jewish strangers. Some of them still carry their thick staffs, and they look as if they will start to use them. But the enthusiasm of the women confuses them. Much talking and arguing ensues. The Samaritan woman drags Jesus from household to household and introduces Jesus to as many of the women as she can. James and Thomas talk with several of the shepherds about the journey from Galilee. And Thaddeus and Judas question the men about raising sheep in such a dry area. John greets Rina with a hug and starts a game with her and the other children. The men are mollified but still wary, but the friendliness of the strangers draws them in. And the testimony of the Samaritan woman provokes a lot of questions.

And so, the Jews are invited to stay overnight. The women make a pot of stew with chicken and vegetables and another large pot of barley and onion. One of the shepherds brings out a jar of wine. Mary and Joanna make a mound of flatbreads brushed with olive oil, and Judas piles a platter high with dates. Peter throws nuts in the air for the children, encouraging them to catch them in their mouths before they fall to the ground. Two of the eldest shepherds talk long into the night with Jesus and John, and the woman from the well, whose name is Pasi, never leaves Jesus' side. After the meal, many of the women sit with Joanna and Mary and ask questions not only about Jesus and his teaching but about their lives in Galilee. Finally, when the moon has passed completely overhead, everyone goes home and the travelers wrap themselves up in their cloaks and fall asleep.

The next morning, Jesus and his companions awake early, eat a quick breakfast, and prepare to leave. Realizing that they are going, the shepherds, who have been checking on their flocks, approach them. The eldest shepherd gives a slight bow to Jesus and says, "Rabbi, we would be honored if you could stay a little longer. We have many neighbors who would benefit from your wisdom. We can gather them quickly. You have words of truth that we have never heard before."

"I am sorry," says Jesus. "We must arrive in Jerusalem in good time for the Passover, and so we cannot stay. We are grateful for your invitation and the hospitality, but we must be gone. We will pray for you as we travel. I know you have the strength and wisdom to speak to your neighbors. The Spirit of God is with you because you have accepted me."

Crestfallen, the shepherds rouse their wives, and all say goodbye to one another.

X V

Two days later, the group is almost to the outskirts of Jerusalem. Joanna is walking with Matthew when he points to a path leading to the east. "It seems strange to be passing right by," he says. "Usually, we turn here."

"Why?" asks Joanna. "What is down the track?"

"It is the way to Bethany, the home of Martha, Mary, and their brother, Lazarus. But I suppose Jesus doesn't want to visit them trailing all these people. Donkeys and villagers, plus the animals for sacrifice, make a lot of chaos!"

Joanna looks behind her and realizes that even more people from the nearby villages have spread out behind them. There is a parade-like atmosphere, and some have even stripped trees of their palms and are waving them. Some are chanting political slogans, and some are singing psalms.

Soon they arrive at the olive groves overlooking the Kidron Valley and Jerusalem. The limestone walls of the city gleam in the sunshine. They can see crowds streaming through both gates on the eastern wall. As the disciples and the women look down on the city separated from them by the small valley, there is relief on their faces. They have arrived in time!

In contrast, Jesus' face is solemn. The excitement of those who have newly joined them seems to burden rather than invigorate him. He gathers the core group together so that plans can be made. "After we enter the city, I wish to go straight to the temple," Jesus says.

The disciples nod. Just then, Nathaniel and Thaddeus appear leading a small donkey. Someone has put a cloak on its back, and

Thaddeus greets them, saying, "Now, Jesus, you can enter the city properly!"

"Wait. Just a minute, please," says Mary, holding up her hand. "I think that Joanna and I should go ahead to open up the apartment and make sure the rooms are clean. Hopefully, no one else has taken them over. The rooms are on Beit Habad Street near the center of the city. The rooms are on the upper level, above a large spice shop. The crowds will be crushing, so we will hang my blue scarf out the top window so that you will be able to find us."

Peter nods in agreement. "The city is filled to overflowing. It will take us some time to make our way through those crowds." He turns to Jesus. "And what about your mother?"

"Don't worry if my mother is delayed. Passover is still three days away. There is still time for her to get here if she hasn't arrived already."

"Don't stop for provisions," adds Judas to Joanna and Mary. "We will buy food and supplies after we leave the temple. But here is the money for the rent."

The women nod, and Mary, Joanna, and Rina slowly join the stream of people taking the main path that winds down from the olive and palm groves, crosses the valley, and leads up to the Lion's Gate. Jesus and the disciples turn back to the crowd that has followed them. The people surround them and start chanting praises. Jesus quiets them and starts preaching.

The women become part of the slow-moving crowd making its way through the gate. Rina is overwhelmed by the crush of people, the immensity of the limestone walls, and the gigantic stone archway. She clings to Joanna's hand, her eyes getting wider and wider. Having experienced the Passover in Jerusalem before, the women are not quite so overcome, but they, too, join hands to keep from being separated. They are jostled between pilgrims, donkeys, a caravan, and myriads of people selling breads, nuts, and sweets all along the way.

On either side of the entrance, a line of temporary mikvahs is set up. Immense brass bowls are held on tripods, and the water in them is constantly refreshed by a group of women hired by the temple officials.

Mary and Joanna dip their hands in the water and murmur, "Blessed is the Eternal, the God of all creation, who has blessed me with life and sustained me."

Rina copies them, and then all three are swept through the gate. Rina looks up and sees the heavy iron portcullis that can be lowered against an enemy. The loops of ropes that are attached to the pulleys are as thick as her arm, and Roman soldiers lean over the ramparts keeping a close eye on all who enter. Their weapons glint in the sunlight. Scared, Rina ducks her head and clings closely to Joanna.

The road continues past scores of two-story houses, but the Temple Mount can be seen through the gaps. It, too, gleams in the sunshine. All the houses lining the streets have shops on the bottom selling any number of things needed by arrivals: spices, fabrics, clothes, pots, fuel, and water. The noise is incredible. Shouts pile upon shouts: hawkers, shopkeepers, people offering accommodations. Some are selling caged birds. There are live chickens for dinner and doves for the temple sacrifices. Dogs are barking, and donkeys are braying. The dust never has time to completely settle and causes everyone to cough.

After a brief discussion about directions with a woman who is sweeping, they turn onto a side street which is only slightly less crowded. They start craning their necks, looking for the names of the alleyways and small streets they pass. They finally find Beit Habad, and halfway down the street, Mary sees the spice merchant they are looking for. After checking in with him and paying the necessary rent, they make their way through his shop out to the back. They take stairs up to the second-story apartment. As they climb, Mary turns and speaks over her shoulder. "If I hadn't been here with my husband before, I don't think I would have been able to find it!"

They enter the door to their rooms. The shopkeeper and his wife have temporarily moved out all of their belongings. The outer room is empty except for a small table and a bench propped against the wall. Two windows give light. Going into the inner room, they need to wait a moment for their eyes to adjust to the sudden darkness. There is a small clay oven in the corner and two sturdy shelves on the wall. Three wooden stools are stacked in the corner. It is quite dim, with just a small opening in the roof that allows smoke to escape.

"I think if you hadn't been here before," observes Joanna, "the owner would not have kept these rooms for us. We are lucky to have so much space." Sending Rina down below to borrow a bucket and a broom from the shopkeeper, Mary and Joanna right the bench and hang a blue cloth out of one of the windows. Then they both sit down and sag against the wall. They turn to one another and grin. They are here, safe and sound!

XVI

———

Three days later, Joanna stands, arms akimbo, in the outer room. Bundles line the walls, and signs of occupation are everywhere. Walking sticks are propped in the corner, and cloaks are piled next to the bench. Nathaniel and Matthew are sprawled on the floor. It is past noon, and the two men have been left at home to help with preparations.

Joanna gives a snort and issues several orders. "Please, you two, fold and tidy all the belongings and pile them neatly in the other room. Put the walking sticks out on the landing so that Rina can sweep. Then, if you would be so kind, take three of our jugs and go to the well. We will need extra water for cleaning and cooking."

Nathaniel and Matthew roll their eyes at one another but cheerfully follow the directions.

"After that, you can leave and join the others. If you stay here, you will just be in the way," teases Mary. "Oh, and on your way out, ask if the shop owner has any pillows he can spare."

By the time twilight comes, the outer room has been transformed. Cloaks and pillows form a U-shape. The small table is standing in front of the back wall nearest the inner room and has been covered with a cloth. There is some bread on a platter, jugs with wine, and various bowls and plates full of what is needed for the Passover dinner. The smell of roasting lamb fills the room. Bowls of karpas, the bitter herbs, are ready for serving. Several oil lamps and candles cast leaping shadows as air comes through the propped-open windows. Then there is the sound of steady footsteps on the stairs, and Jesus and the disciples enter the room. They are talking enthusiastically, taking off their cloaks, and piling them on the others.

Mary and Joanna come from the inner room with smiles on their faces. Unnoticed, a small woman in black is hidden behind them. As they step apart, the light flickers on the face of Mary, the mother of Jesus. Her face is calm, but there is a mischievous glint in her eyes. Laugh lines surround her eyes, and she waits for Jesus to notice her. John glimpses her first and starts to grin.

As Jesus turns, he catches sight of her. He pushes by John and Thomas, lifts her up in a big hug, and twirls her around. "Mother! You are here. You arrived in time!"

Mary is laughing and swatting at Jesus, trying to get him to let her down. "Yes, Jesus, I am here. Stop making such a fuss."

"When did you arrive?"

"I didn't get here until early this afternoon. One of our party was ill along the way and that delayed us, but we are here now. Emet agreed to accompany me here." She gestures to a capable, sturdy woman who is smiling too.

"Welcome, Emet," says Jesus. "Thank you for bringing my mother safely here." Jesus twirls Mary again, and she giggles.

"Jesus, put me down. Mary, Joanna, and Rina have made us quite welcome, and the Passover feast is almost ready. You should all sit down. It's time to eat."

Joanna notices that Jesus has Mary's eyes, if not her stature. Mary only comes up to his chest, and she has to tilt her head up to speak to him. Jesus clings to her hands and doesn't take his eyes off her face. Ignoring her words, he pulls her forward. "Mother, please, sit here next to me. I have missed you so much, and I have a lot to tell you."

"And I will hear all about it later. Walk Emet to the door so that she can join her family. They are waiting for her down the street."

Emet receives Jesus' blessing, and all say goodbye. Again Jesus urges his mother to sit next to him. She laughs in protest. "Have you ever known me to be seated during the Passover feast? We women have had plenty of time to get to know one another, and we've arranged everything . . . Here, give a place to Mary and Rina. Joanna and I are more than able to serve this small group of rascals. But first make sure that you all wash in preparation for the meal."

She ruffles John's hair as she passes. She and Joanna disappear into the inner room. All line up for the ritual washing. Soon everyone is arranged on either side of Jesus, and the familiar celebration of the Passover feast begins.

Jesus recites the familiar prayer: "Blessed are you, O Lord our God, King of the universe, who have created the fruit of the vine . . . And you, O Lord our God, have given us festival days for joy, this feast of the unleavened bread, the time of our deliverance, in remembrance of the departure from Egypt. Blessed are you, O Lord our God, who have kept us alive, sustained us, and enabled us to enjoy this season."

The others echo the prescribed response. "Blessed are you, O Lord our God, who have created the fruit of the vine. Blessed are you, O Lord our God, who have kept us alive, sustained us, and enabled us to enjoy this season."

There is contentment and peace in the room as the ritual prayers and feasting continue, but Joanna notices that this Passover celebration is also unusually solemn. Jesus chooses his words carefully and prays them with a great depth of feeling, his face growing more and more serious. Some of the disciples cast uneasy glances at him, and only Rina seems unaware of the strange atmosphere. The peace seems fragile. As the meal ends, everything is cleared away. Minutes later, coming into the room, Joanna wipes her hands on the cloth at her waist. She notices that there is an empty place and realizes that Judas is gone and that most conversation has died away. The usual post-Passover celebration chatter is missing. Jesus' mother sits down in Judas's vacated place, and as Joanna starts to squeeze in, too, Jesus stands. He walks to a bundle piled in the corner and pulls out a rough, woven prayer shawl. Turning back to the group, he ceremoniously places the shawl over his head and waits for a deeper silence. The disciples are confused with this break in tradition, and all are struck by the grave yet tender look on Jesus' face.

"Joanna," he says. "Could you please bring me two cups of wine and some unleavened bread also?"

James gets up to help her and brings a platter with the bread, while Joanna brings up the cups of wine. They place them in front of Jesus and return, James to his seat, Joanna standing at the back. As they walk back, several of the candles gutter out and the room becomes darker, the shadows larger.

"I have greatly desired to share this Passover with you before I suffer," Jesus says softly.

There are small sounds of objections and dismay from the disciples. But the women make no sound, keeping their eyes fixed on Jesus.

"No, I tell you, from this time on I will not drink of the fruit of the vine until the kingdom of God comes." Jesus picks up the bread, tears it in two, and lifts the pieces so that all can see. "We give you thanks, Father, for the grain of the fields."

Peter murmurs an assent.

Jesus continues, "This is my body, which will be given for you." As he speaks, Jesus hands the bread to either side. "Do this in memory of me."

Each follower reverently tears off a small piece, eats it, and passes it to the next person. Joanna sees that Mary Magdalene and John are weeping. Mary, Jesus' mother, does not cry, but her eyes never leave Jesus' face. Joanna can barely swallow the small piece of bread as dismay rises within her. Joanna carefully collects the fragments onto a plate and puts it on the small table.

Then Jesus lifts both cups. "We give you thanks, Father, for the fruit of the vine."

This time all say, "Amen."

"Take this drink, the blood of the new covenant, and share it among yourselves. Do this in memory of me."

He passes one cup to one side, one cup to the other. Each one takes a drink and passes it to the next in line. Solemnly, James offers the cup to Joanna, and she finishes it, putting the cup on the table. Mary finishes the other cup. It is so quiet in the room they can hear each other breathing.

Then Jesus lowers the prayer shawl to his shoulders and says abruptly, "We must go to the garden and spend the night in prayer to prepare for the coming days. Gather your things."

The disciples pick up their cloaks, unsure of what has just taken place. The women stay in their places, not sure what to do next. Jesus walks over to his mother and draws her to her feet. As the disciples start leaving the room, he says, "Mother, may I please have my childhood blessing?"

Mary smiles. "You haven't outgrown it?"

"I will never outgrow it."

Mary smiles again, and with a faltering but determined voice she pronounces the blessing she has given since he was a child. "The Lord is your guard and your shade; at your right side he stands. By day the sun shall not smite you, nor the moon in the night, and may his angels who sang at your birth watch over you."

And then they say together, "Lest you dash your foot against a stone."

Jesus embraces Mary for a long moment and then reluctantly turns to Joanna. "Take care of my mother, Joanna. She is precious to me, to all of us." Jesus embraces his mother one more time, smiles gravely at Mary Magdalene, Joanna, and Rina, and leaves the upper room. The disciples follow him out.

Joanna turns and picks up the empty cups and takes them into the other room. Jesus' mother walks over to Mary Magdalene, who is still crying, and places her hand on her head to comfort her.

"I don't know why I am crying," Mary Magdalene says.

Mary murmurs words of comfort, but when she turns, her face is deathly pale. She goes and picks up the platter of bread fragments. She gently touches them, cradling the platter in her arms. Her eyes glisten. Mary Magdalene closes her eyes and folds her hands. In the other room, Joanna and Rina silently do the dishes. Worry and tension make the small chore difficult. Soon the women are asleep in the inner room, covered with their cloaks. The hours pass. There are just a few embers of fire left in the brazier. Mats are spread in the outer room, waiting for the men's return. The night sky wheels above. Suddenly, they are startled awake by pounding steps on the stairs and across the landing. Alarmed, they wrap their cloaks around them. Rina quickly lights a small oil lamp as James bursts into the outer room. He is exhausted and shaking with fear. As he sinks to the floor, Mary Magdalene stoops next to him. "James, James what has happened?"

"Is my brother here? Where are they? Are any of them here?"

"What do you mean?" asks Mary Magdalene. James only moans, and Mary shakes him. "James! Tell us. What is the matter? What has happened?"

James can barely speak. "You all saw that Judas left during the meal, didn't you? Well, Judas told the temple soldiers where we were. He led them to us. He betrayed us all." James shakes his head in disbelief. "They arrested Jesus while we were praying. The temple guards and elders came and took Jesus away!"

"Took him? Took him where?" Joanna's voice is shaking.

"To the high priest."

Jesus' mother's hands are trembling, but her voice is calm. "And what was the charge?"

"I think they accused him of blasphemy. I stood in the back of the crowd because I was afraid of being recognized. There was a huge argument, and then they sent him to the Roman procurator. I followed along with the rest of the crowd. From what I could hear, they also accused Jesus of incitement against the government. After listening, Pilate refused to make a judgment."

"But that's a good thing, isn't it?" cries Joanna. "Surely they will release him!"

James gives a cry and rocks on his heels, covering his face with his hands. "No, this is a nightmare that will never end. Now they are taking Jesus to Herod Agrippa to be judged."

The women cry in disbelief and horror.

"Where are the rest of the disciples? Have some of them been arrested too?" Mary Magdalene asks.

"No, while they were busy arresting Jesus, the rest of us ran away. We hid among the trees and watched them march him off."

"Ran away? You left him? You just left him?" Crying, Mary Magdalene starts striking James. He puts up his hands to ward her off but does not push her away.

"Some of us followed after in the darkness. We didn't think we could help if we were arrested too. I saw Peter in Pilate's courtyard, but when I heard that Jesus was being taken to Herod, I ran back here to see if the others had come back."

Jesus' mother stands frozen in place. The only movement is the trembling of her clenched hands. She does not utter a word, but her face is full of pain. Rina cowers near the far wall, crying. Joanna goes to her and pulls her close. "You said they are taking him to Herod? So are they taking him to Herod's palace here in Jerusalem?"

James nods.

Joanna immediately makes up her mind. "I will go. I must go. I know the palace. I've been there many times. Maybe there is something I can do. Maybe I can help. They won't hurt me; they know me!"

"Joanna," says Mary. "What can you possibly do?"

"I don't know, but I can't stay here while they bring him before Herod." Joanna clasps her hands together to keep them from trembling. "He is a stupid man, a paranoid man. He is corrupt and a Roman lackey." Jesus' mother's face turns an ashen gray. Joanna continues, "Maybe I can testify on Jesus' behalf. Herod will recognize me—maybe he will listen!"

"They won't let you testify! You're a woman." Mary Magdalene shakes her head in despair and grabs Joanna by the arm.

She shrugs herself free. "But I must try. Maybe I can find some of the disciples. We can't just do nothing. Please, watch over Rina and Mary. I'll be back as soon as I can. James, come with me!"

Joanna dashes out the door and down the stairs as Mary Magdalene reaches out again to try and restrain her. James follows. Jesus' mother continues to stand, frozen in place. Dawn begins to streak the sky as James and Joanna run through the streets. Not many are up this early, but as they get closer to the palace, small groups of men appear along the way, milling about and arguing. As they turn down the main street in front of the palace, they have to stop. There is a sizable crowd blocking the main gate, and the bars are lowered. The torches lighting the entrance are have not been extinguished yet, sending smoke stuttering up into the sky. Some of the palace guards, with their lances lowered, stand in front of the gate shouting at the crowd to disperse—that there is no more room inside. More soldiers peer over the wall. James shoves his way through the crowd with Joanna close behind him. As they reach the gate, the crowd surges, and she and James are separated. One of the guards shoves her back. Joanna cries James's name, but he doesn't hear her. For a moment, she can't think, then she remembers a different way to try to get into the palace. She frantically exits the crowd and runs around the palace perimeter until she reaches a small door that she knows leads into the kitchen area.

She waits until she sees a servant leaving the door ajar as he dumps some waste water into the street. She darts in. Trying to avoid being noticed, she walks quickly past the ovens and fires and around tables piled with fruits and vegetables being prepared for the morning meal. She slips through the far door, crosses a hall, and comes to a portico looking out onto a small inner courtyard. She can hear the shouts of the crowd on the other side of the wall. Desperately, she tries to remember which hallway leads from this small courtyard to the main one. Seeing a doorway, she decides to take a chance and starts to run when suddenly, someone grabs her by the arm. It is Chuza!

"Joanna," he hisses, "what are you doing here? Who let you in?"

"Chuza, I didn't expect to see you here! I got in through the kitchen." She shakes her head. "Never mind. You have to help me. I need to see Jesus. I have come to help him." She strains to break his hold on her.

"What are you talking about?"

"Let me go—I must talk to Herod. Jesus is an innocent man. He is not dangerous. He is no threat."

"Are you out of your mind? What does all this have to do with you? I can't believe that you are mixed up in it. What do you think will happen to you? They'll arrest you too."

"But Jesus hasn't done anything! He preaches about the kingdom of God. He calls God 'Abba,' his Father. He is a peaceful man. He is a good man."

She struggles even harder.

"Joanna, stop! You're hysterical. You don't know what you are saying."

"No, you must let me go!" She scratches and kicks him. "Let me go!"

Chuza picks her up and half drags her back into the kitchen. She struggles and yells. He shoves her into a large storeroom and slams the door. He is hesitant to leave her, but a servant comes looking for him, saying he is needed. He shoots the bolt in firmly. "I'm doing this for your own good," he shouts. "When this farce is over, I will send someone to let you out. It is too dangerous to have you wandering around embarrassing me. I really think you have lost your mind!"

Joanna paces up and down, her hands clenched. Her thoughts race one after another. She looks around the storeroom. Vegetables are piled high in baskets. There is shelving all along the back wall and sacks of grains near the floor. Crockery and dishes are piled high on the upper shelves. Near the ceiling are two small windows propped open for ventilation. As she paces, she can hear shouts from the crowd in the courtyard. The crowd starts chanting, but she can't quite make out the words. She decides to try and see what is happening. She starts to climb the shelving to get to the nearest window. As she gets near the top shelf, the shelving teeters and shakes, the dishes start to shake and fall, and finally, everything crashes down. Joanna is thrown down, her head hits the floor, and everything goes black.

XVII

Joanna wakes up. Someone is bathing her head with water. When she tries to open her eyes, the room spins. "My lady, my lady," someone says. "Please stay still. You have been unconscious a long time. Chuza sent me. How did you come to be here? How were you hurt?"

Finally, Joanna recognizes the voice. It is Sandor. She is too disoriented to speak. Her head throbs, and half of her face is badly bruised. Her left eye is almost swollen shut, and one whole side of her body aches.

As Sandor continues to bathe her face, she looks around, dazed, and gradually starts to remember. "This is Herod's palace, isn't it? I tried to climb up the shelves to see out the window, but I fell."

"But what are you doing here? And why did Chuza lock you in?"

"I came to try and help Jesus."

"You wanted to see a criminal? But what do you have to do with such a man?" Sandor's face is wreathed in concern. He continues to gently clean off the dried blood as best he can. "What could make you come here at a time like this?"

Joanna winces and tries to sit up. "Oh, Sandor. It is a long, long story. It is good to see you, but the story is too long to tell now. Do you know what happened between Herod and Jesus? Did he free him?"

Sandor looks away, reluctant to say anything. "No, Herod sent Jesus back to Pilate. He didn't want the responsibility of judgment in front of such an angry crowd."

"So is Jesus in jail? Will I be able to see him, do you think?" She sways as she tries to rise.

"My lady, sit back. You have been sorely hurt. Please wait here while I get you something to eat. I'll bring only soft foods."

"Yes, maybe some food and water will help with the dizziness. But then I will have to leave."

Sandor comes back with bread soaked in milk. Joanna eats it gingerly, since the side of her face is so badly bruised. The inside of her mouth is raw, and she can barely open her lips. She refuses the wine he offers. "Thank you, Sandor. That is much better. I think I'm strong enough to walk now." The dizziness has eased somewhat. She stands up but loses her balance and sinks back onto the floor. She touches her face, checking the swelling and bruising. But still determined, she asks, "Tell me, where is the Roman jail? I have never been there."

"My lady, really, you must rest. It is almost sundown now, and you can barely stand. You will not be allowed in the jail until tomorrow. I have been tending to you for most of the day."

"It's really that late?"

"Besides, why do you want to go to the jail?"

"To visit Jesus and see if he needs anything. His disciples are probably there too. Maybe we can decide what to do next."

Sandor takes both of Joanna's hands and looks into her eyes. "Do you have a place to stay in the city?"

Joanna nods.

"Then you must return there. Really, you need to go back there. It is almost nightfall." Sandor's face is full of compassion and worry.

"No, Sandor. I must go to the jail."

Sandor pauses for a moment. He doesn't speak for a long moment. Finally, he says, "Joanna, this has been a long and terrible day. The palace has been full of many rumors. But Herod received a final report from Pontius Pilate, and now all of Jerusalem knows of it." Sandor takes both of Joanna's hands. "I have terrible news. Jesus was crucified as ordered early this afternoon. The Romans put him to death."

Joanna stares at Sandor. "He was crucified?" Her voice drops. "On a cross?"

Sandor nods.

Joanna is unaware that tears are falling down her face. "But that can't be true. Who did it? How could they do it?"

"He was accused of blasphemy by the Sanhedrin. The sentence was carried out immediately. The Roman guard took him up to Golgatha and crucified him there. It was a mercy he died fairly quickly. He has already been buried because of the Sabbath."

"But I don't understand. How can he be dead?" Her face crumples. "I believed in him. I believed that he was the Son of God. It can't all be over, it just can't." She lays her head on Sandor's shoulder and sobs. She cannot bear to think of Jesus being so cruelly treated. Nothing makes sense. How could God be murdered? Then she remembers her last promise to Jesus: to take care of his mother. How will she ever be able to face her? Guilt floods her. Sandor tries fruitlessly to comfort her.

Much later, Joanna walks through the streets still filled with festival crowds. She walks slowly, and every once in a while, she sits down against a wall for a moment. Whenever she emerges from the shadows, people walking by stare at her bruised face, but she is unaware of them. Her whole body shakes with fatigue. When she finally reaches the spice merchant's house, she climbs the stairs. She tries to open the door, but it is locked. She knocks and calls out. John opens the door and draws her in. The disciples are huddled about the room. John takes Joanna's hands and kisses her.

"We are so glad you have returned! But your face!"

Joanna looks at him dully. "Is it true, John? Is Jesus really dead? How did this happen?"

John swallows several times. "Yes, it's true. After the final verdict, I came back here to tell Mary and his mother.

"You must tell me, John. You must tell me everything."

"We knew we couldn't let him go to his death alone, so Mary and I decided to follow him. We tried to make his mother stay here, but she refused. We so wanted to spare her the sight of Jesus' pain. Joanna—they even made him carry his own cross, and the soldiers beat him every time he fell!"

Joanna covers her mouth in horror.

"There was so much blood. All we could do was stand at the foot of the cross. He would look at us, but it was difficult for him to speak. He did ask me to take care of his mother. He hung on the cross about three hours. His breath became louder and louder, slower and more labored. His pain was horrifying. After he died, the soldiers told us we had to take him down right away because of the Sabbath. We didn't know what to do."

John takes a deep breath, hesitates, and then continues, unaware that tears are streaming down his face. "An elder from the temple offered his own tomb for the burial. It was very kind." John breaks down, and several moments pass until he can continue. Finally, he says, "So we carried him down the hill and put him in the newly hollowed cave. Mary Magdalene and I had a hard time persuading Jesus' mother to leave the tomb. She just knelt with her face against the stone that was used to block the entrance. Her grief was awful to witness."

Joanna looks around the room at the disciples, but the men look away, shame evident on every face. She knows why now. They had not stood beside Jesus; they had abandoned him. Peter is huddled in the corner with his back to everyone and won't look at her at all. She wants to yell and scream at them for being cowards, but suddenly she is so tired she can no longer stand up. She goes into the inner room. Mary, Jesus' mother, is asleep on a pallet in the corner. Mary Magdalene is sitting next to Rina, trying to get her to eat.

Rina jumps up and hugs Joanna tightly. "I was afraid you were never coming back!"

Joanna clings to her, unable to speak. She starts to sink to the floor. Mary stands and eases her down. Mary seems to have aged ten years and moves as if her bones and muscles ache as badly as Joanna's. She pats Joanna and says slowly, "You are back with us. That's good. We have been so worried. We feared that . . . your poor face."

"It's not important. There was nothing I could do. I couldn't do anything. I was locked in a storeroom and was knocked unconscious. Oh, Mary, how could they have killed him? How could God have let this happen?"

"I don't know. It is horrible, absolutely awful." They cling to one another. "The men are so frightened; they are afraid they will be next. A neighbor told us that they are looking for the men who followed Jesus, so we women are the only ones who can go out. They aren't looking for us."

Joanna turns and looks at Mary, who is sleeping. "I'm so sorry I left. I should have stayed and fulfilled my promise. His mother. How can she bear this?"

"I don't know. She stayed with him. She never turned away."

Joanna murmurs, "I should never have left her or Rina. I promised Jesus that I would take care of her! I shouldn't have left!"

"Joanna, it's not your fault. There was nothing you could have done. There was nothing any of us could do."

"But I could have been there. I could have seen him one last time! There was so much I needed to tell him. Now he will never know that I believed in him as God's Son."

"I know, I know. What are we going to do?" Mary sobs. They cling to one another.

Finally, Joanna gets up and, bending stiffly, looks carefully at Mary's sleeping face and straightens the cloak over her. "Her breathing is very slow."

"We have given her valerian tea to help her sleep. Perhaps I should drink some too. Every time I close my eyes, I see his poor hands and feet. They even pierced him with a lance. He was in such pain! What will become of us? What are we without him?" Joanna, Rina, and Mary clutch at one another.

The next morning, Mary Magdalene tries to make some kind of plan. The men are still in a stupor, so she talks about it with Joanna. "Early tomorrow morning, you and I need to go to the grave to anoint Jesus' body. It has been untended too long as it is. We should leave early, before Mary wakes up. She will want to go, but I don't think she should have to face it. It will be a comfort to her if we perform the task. John and Rina can keep her company while we are gone. Maybe she won't even wake if we get up early enough."

"Mary, I can't go. I can't leave his mother and Rina again. I need to keep my promise."

"But what of our Lord? We can't leave him without the proper prayers and burial rites."

"I'm so sorry, Mary, but I must stay here. My duty is to the living now. Jesus is gone, but his mother needs me."

"Of course, you are right. I would take some of the disciples, but they can't be seen going to the tomb. There may be soldiers around looking for them. The shopkeeper's wife across the road offered to go with me as a mitzvah, and her daughter will too. But it will be hard for me to face this without you."

"How will you bear it?"

"As long as I can serve him." She smiles and cries at the same time.

"But the stone? How will you get into the tomb?"

"I don't know," says Mary wearily, "but I must try."

They hug one another. Joanna turns to check on Jesus' mother. She leans over, brushes aside her hair, and adjusts her cloak. She stifles a sob as she notices the tear tracks that have dried on Mary's face. Exhausted again, head throbbing, she lays down to rest next to her. Rina lays a cold cloth over the bruises on her face. Joanna falls into a restless sleep.

Joanna wakes up as she hears Jesus' mother stir. Turning over, she sees Rina blowing on the brazier embers. Joanna gets up and gives her a long hug before squatting down next to Mary. Mary's eyes open, and she recognizes Joanna. Joanna grasps Mary's hand as the tears start to flow.

"My son, my son, my only son," she keens.

Joanna holds her as she rocks back and forth. Filled with desolation, there is nothing she can say.

Later, Rina and Joanna warm bread and cut some small bits of cheese. Mary refuses to eat, but some of the disciples are hungry. John encourages Jesus' mother to come out to the other room. He sits next to her on the bench, holding her hand, and encourages her to take some watered wine.

As Joanna passes out food and drink, she overhears John murmuring, "Mother, mother, I will be a son to you now."

Some accept the food but still can't meet Joanna's eyes. Peter refuses the food altogether and continues to rock back and forth. She hugs him briefly around the shoulders, then returns to the other room. She sits down next to Rina, who chooses a salve from the medical bag. Joanna winces as Rina gently daubs the swelling and the bruises. The minutes go slowly by. No one says much. Exhausted by grief, all go to sleep early. Early the next morning, Joanna scarcely stirs as Mary Magdalene leaves to go to the tomb.

XVIII

At midmorning, Peter sits on the top step of the stairs staring off into space. Suddenly, there is the sound of someone pounding up the stairs, and Mary Magdalene appears. She is flushed with excitement. She rushes past Peter, grabs him with astonishing strength, and drags him after her. They burst into the room. Peter is totally confused as Mary tries to catch her breath. Startled, everyone stares at her. Finally she gasps, "I have seen the Lord!"

Peter grabs her by the shoulders. "What? What are you saying?"

"I saw Jesus. It was Jesus, luminous and different, but I am sure. It was him—his voice, his pierced hands. He walked with me; he spoke to me."

Anguished, John blurts, "It's not possible! What about the tomb?" He can barely speak.

"It is empty. Empty except for the burial cloths. When we got there, the stone was rolled away. Frightened, the other women ran away. I will never forget it. I stared and stared at the emptiness. I couldn't believe that someone had taken the body. Still in shock, I sat down nearby. Then I saw a man. I thought he was a gardener, but he was Jesus. He called me by name."

"But that is impossible!" Thomas is adamant, shaking his head in denial.

Mary Magdalene raises her voice, and it rings as clear as a bell, her face glowing. "Listen—listen to me! You must listen! Jesus himself told me to come and tell you. He wants you to know he is alive! He stood right next to me."

These words electrify everyone. John and Peter dash down the stairs to see for themselves, the possibility of danger forgotten. The rest of the disciples, Joanna, and Rina swirl around Mary Magdalene, talking excitedly over one another. No one notices that Jesus' mother has entered from the other room. Finally, Joanna remembers and turns to look for Mary. The radiance on her face slices through the noise. Everyone turns to face her.

Holding out her hands in prayer and lifting her eyes to heaven, she says, "He has come to the help of his servant Israel, for he has remembered his promise of mercy, the promise he made to our forbearers, to Abraham and Sarah and his children forever." Lowering her hands, she says, "Jesus is the promise. He has risen. He is the Christ."

Joanna feels her knees buckle, and she sinks to the floor with Rina by her side. She is overcome with wonder. One by one, the disciples kneel and place their foreheads on the ground. A deep and joyful peace fills the room. No one speaks for a very long time.

X V I V

It is twenty years later. Two elderly women gossip comfortably as they slowly walk down a street that slopes to a harbor visible in the distance. The sea is a bright aqua blue. One- and two-story houses line the street and are sandwiched between the bright blue of the sea and the softer blue of the sky. Seagulls fly overhead, and the white houses glisten. The harbor at Ephesus is a beautiful sight.

The younger of the two women asks, "Has she really been here that long?"

"Yes, she came with John and Jesus' mother about two years after the crucifixion. It was about twenty years ago. They lived together in a small house in the hills outside town until Mary died. John would go out preaching and do missionary work, returning often. Joanna and Rina, her daughter, would attend to Mary and keep house. Almost every day, she and Mary would invite anyone who wanted to come to hear stories about Jesus. Their courtyard would become quite crowded. Mary died twelve years ago. We still feel her loss. She was the most gracious and loving person. After her death, John continued his travels.

"What happened to Joanna and Rina?"

"Then Joanna married Darelos. He is one of the most prominent shipbuilders in Ephesus. He waited a long time for Joanna, because she wouldn't leave Mary. For a long time, she also practiced as a midwife. She attended my grandniece's birth, and it was a hard, long delivery. But that was a while ago. Now Rina tends to the women of the neighborhood. Joanna and Darelos hold services in their courtyard every week, and all are invited."

"I am so excited to finally meet her. To think she was really there and knew Jesus."

"I know. But sometimes her stories sound unbelievable, and some of the teachings are hard to follow, but they certainly give you a lot to think about."

The women turn into an archway leading into a courtyard. They slow, as there are several people in front of them. Joanna, her husband, Darelos, and Rina are standing at the archway welcoming latecomers. They chat briefly with each person, and several people kiss Joanna's hands. Her energetic faith is evident in the brightness of her eyes and the warmth of her greetings. Rina is still reserved, but with a confident, straight posture. Darelos stands behind Joanna, resting his hand on the small of her back. He is obviously proud of her. He has an amiable face, weather-beaten and rough.

"Greetings, Sarah. Welcome." Joanna greets the elder woman with a swift clasp of the hands.

"Greetings to you too. I am sorry that we have missed the communal meal. This is my sister, who is visiting for several weeks. She has wanted to meet you for a long time. You are famous, you know!"

Joanna laughs. "That's better than being infamous. You both are most welcome." The women turn and look for places to sit.

The courtyard is large, with high, lime-washed walls. Palm trees in containers provide shade, and vines snake up the house, softening the gleaming white. Wooden benches and a scattering of stools face a large table on a low dais at the far end of the courtyard. The benches have been rearranged and are divided in two by an aisle. Almost all the seats are filled. There are about fifty people in attendance, most Greeks, but some Jews, and even some Cretans from a docked ship in the harbor. The two sisters are late, and the remnants of the agape meal have been whisked away.

Joanna, Rina, and Mary are not the only ones who made their way to Ephesus. Sandor is arranging a white cloth on the table. He is older, of course, but still deft and quick. After he finishes, he comes down the center aisle, smiling at his wife and their passel of children sitting in the front row. After a few moments, when no one else comes to the gate, Darelos and Rina take their places in the front row. The assembly quiets. Joanna picks up a platter of bread from a small table at the end of the aisle, and Sandor carries a tray with two large cups and a flask of wine. When they stand at the end of the aisle, the crowd stands, and Rina begins to lead a song of praise. Joanna and Sandor process down. When they reach the table, they both bow slightly and go around to either side. They place the bread and wine on the table and bow deeply, kissing the table.

Sandor begins the prayers. "Thou, O Lord Almighty, hast created all things for the sake of thy name, hast given food and drink to the children of men for enjoyment, but to us thou hast granted spiritual food and drink for eternal life through Jesus, thy servant."

Joanna continues. "For all these things we thankfully praise thee, because thou art powerful. Thine is the glory forever. Amen."

"Amen," echoes the gathering.

Sandor walks to the front of the altar and says, "There are two ways: one of life and one of death! And there is a great difference between the two ways. On the one hand, the way of life is this: first, you will love the God who made you; second, you will love your neighbor as yourself. And concerning these matters, the teaching is this: speak well of the ones speaking badly of you and pray for your enemies, for what merit is there if you love the ones loving you? Do not even the unbelievers do the same thing? To anyone asking you for anything, give it and do not ask for it back; for to all, the Father wishes to give these things from his own free gifts." Sandor opens his hands in prayer. "Blessed is the one giving according to the commandment, for he is blameless. Amen."

The crowd again repeats, "Amen." As the gathering sits, Sandor goes to the chair at the side of the altar, and Joanna walks to the front of the table. She moves slowly, and her fragility, which was masked by her warm manner, becomes evident. She addresses the group.

"Many of you know well the commandments God our Father gave the Jews. And these commandments are the foundation of a life in the Spirit. But the commands that Jesus gives us are not additions to those commandments but rather an infusion of light and love into the meaning of these commandments. Caring for one another is the most important of all."

Joanna pauses, swaying a little on her feet. She reaches out to steady herself against the table. She continues, "Because there are so many newcomers today, perhaps I should paint a small picture of Jesus as he was when he walked among us. The question I get asked the most is 'What was Jesus like?' She grins. "Well, he was a man a little taller than me, with brown hair and a brown beard. His hands were calloused from work, and his feet were the feet of a pilgrim. He preached, he taught, he healed, he laughed, he played with children, he shivered in the rain, and he wanted to draw everyone to his heavenly Father. And he was always praying."

Joanna draws a deep breath and continues, hesitantly and thoughtfully. "But what was he like? He wasn't like anyone." She pauses to think. "It is very hard to explain. There was a stillness in him, depths you couldn't reach. And when he spoke, he spoke from that stillness. It was as if he knew something you couldn't know, while all the time knowing you better than you knew yourself. He was always trying to give himself away. His love of others was infinite."

She pauses. "And if you opened yourself up—if you believed in that gift—you received that love pouring out. There were miracles large and small, healed relationships, and joy. But most people he encountered wouldn't or couldn't open themselves up to that love. His sayings were very hard. And I understand, because that's the way I was for a long time." She hesitates before continuing. "I chose not to hear. I chose not to see." Joanna pauses. "And all the while he was preaching and healing, he was an image of the compassion and mercy of God. And he was preparing to die, according to his Father's will. For me, for you. So that magnificent stillness was mingled with sorrow as well as joy. It was hard for his mother, Mary, to stand witness. She more than anyone understood it and accepted it. But he was still her son, her baby boy. She used to say that he was like a mixture of gold, frankincense, and myrrh. Gold for divinity, frankincense for prayer, and myrrh for suffering."

Joanna sags, suddenly running out of energy, and goes to sit down. Rina and Darelos share looks of concern. Sandor goes over to her and whispers, and Joanna shakes her head no and accepts Sandor's help walking over to the table. Sandor takes a step back, and Joanna stands before the bread and wine placed at the center of the table. Joanna takes the bread and offers a small piece to Sandor and takes one herself. They both eat a morsel of bread. Then Joanna takes one of the cups and offers it to Sandor. Then they both drink. Sandor bows to Joanna and takes the platters of bread and hands one to each side of the aisle. Each person in the assembly reverently takes a piece of bread and passes it to the person next to them. Sandor does the same with the cups.

Two people stand at the back of the assembly, collect the plates, and place them on the small table, and Joanna and Sandor return to their seats. After several moments of silence, Joanna and Sandor return to the back of the table and face the group. Joanna begins to pray, "By your prayers and your almsgiving and all your deeds . . ."

Suddenly, Joanna sags in a faint, and Sandor catches her to keep her from falling. Darelos and Rina jump up and, holding her, support her as they take her into the house. As she is led into the house, Joanna can hear Sandor finishing the prayer: "By your prayers and your almsgiving and all your deeds, so do as you have been commanded in the gospel of our Lord. Await his coming and the resurrection of the dead in peace and charity to one another. Amen."

Darelos and Rina place her on her bed. There is one high window on the wall, and it sends a dim shaft of light into the room. Out of consideration, the crowd in the courtyard slips away quickly after the closing prayer, except for some close friends, who sit in prayerful vigil. As Darelos goes to get a pitcher of water, Rina gently removes Joanna's outer garment and removes her veil, drawing the blanket up. Carefully folding the veil, she stares at her mother's face. Joanna's hair is quite gray, and her face is wrinkled from smiling and laughing so much. Her breathing is labored. Her fingers clutch at the covering. Rina kneels at her side, rubbing the familiar, gnarled fingers. Gradually, Joanna relaxes and lets go of the blanket. Darelos reenters the room and lifts her head so that she can take a sip of water. Joanna's eyes signal her thanks, but she is too weak to speak. Darelos and Rina begin to pray in earnest, their prayers mixed with tears. Joanna looks at them both and tries to smile, but it is too much effort.

Throughout the rest of the afternoon, she can barely hear the voices around her. She keeps looking up at the shaft of light as darkness descends inch by inch. Images drift through her mind. Her mother and father, the disciples walking in front of her on the road, Jesus preaching, Rina as a little girl. Darelos laughing at her jokes. The first cries of countless babies. The crowds.

It is sunset, and Joanna looks at the beloved faces one more time. She closes her eyes, and she is back in the garden in Magdala. She can hear the rush of water and wind. The water . . . the wind . . . the cooing of the doves. She can feel the love of so many who have loved her, of the many she has loved. Feelings and memory weave together with her family's prayers until finally, everything is still and dark.

Endnotes

1. Joanna is only mentioned twice in the New Testament. In Luke 8:3, she is listed among the women who minister to Jesus' temporal needs. She is never mentioned as being at the foot of the cross in any of the Gospels, and it is only in Luke 24:10 that she is described as accompanying Mary Magdalene and others to the tomb with spices to anoint Jesus' body. In this account, the women return and witness to the resurrection, but the disciples do not believe them. In the Eastern Orthodox tradition, Joanna is honored as Saint Joanna the Myrrhbearer and is commemorated along with several other women. Her feast is celebrated on the "Sunday of the Myrrhbearers," two Sundays after the Orthodox Easter. There is some discussion by scholars that the woman Junia mentioned in Paul's Letter to the Romans (16:17) is actually Joanna, since it was commonplace for Hebrews to have their native name and to use its Roman equivalent when dealing with officials and bureaucracy

2. Some may be surprised that the practice of a cesarean birth could result in the survival of mother or child in the ancient Middle East. There are references from the Roman period that state it was common among the Jews for a mother to recover from a caesarean section. This evidence is contained in rabbinical reports dating from the second century AD, and of verbal discussions which took place rather earlier. These discussions suggest that there was already a long-standing tradition of practicing the operation. This speaks to the surgical skill of midwives, since infections and fevers were commonplace and often deadly. Further information is contained in the treatise *Gynecology* by Soranus (98–138 AD). Born in Ephesus, he practiced as a physician in Alexandria. His work was first translated in 1886, and he was also an expert on skin

diseases and treatments (Soranus, *Soranus' Gynecology*, translated by Owsei Temkin et al. [Baltimore: The Johns Hopkins University Press, 1991]).

3. At the end of the novel, I chose to place Mary, Joanna, and the apostle John in Ephesus, Turkey. This choice is based on visions of the German mystic Anne Catherine Emmerich recorded in the early nineteenth century. She maintained that the apostle John continued to take care of Mary for the rest of her life. After one of her visions, she described the location of their home in a small building outside Ephesus: "Mary did not live in Ephesus itself, but in the country near it . . . Mary's dwelling was on a hill to the left of the road from Jerusalem, some three and half hours from Ephesus. This hill slopes steeply towards Ephesus; the city, as one approaches it from the southeast, seems to lie on rising ground . . . Narrow paths lead southwards to a hill near the top of which is an uneven plateau, some half hour's journey." In 1881, a small, ancient stone building was discovered on Mt. Koressos, outside Ephesus, by a French priest who had been searching for any sign of the house according to the Emmerich description. Since then it has become a popular pilgrimage site, even though the Catholic Church has not officially determined its authenticity (Izabele Aslan, "House of the Virgin Mary in Ephesus," February 13, 2022 [https://turkisharchaeonews.net/object/house-virgin-mary-ephesus]).

4. The description of the liturgy at the end of the book is taken from historical accounts of the ancient church. Believers gathered once a week on Sundays and shared an agape meal. This meal was usually followed by a eucharistic or thanksgiving service. The words of the liturgy are from the *Didache*, the oldest example of church prayers, dated somewhere around 60 AD (R. C. D. Jasper and G. J. Cuming, *Prayers of the Eucharist: Early and Reformed* [Collegeville, MN: Liturgical, 1990], 20–24).